The Dragon Lord's Secretary
Nicole Petit

THE DRAGON LORD'S SECRETARY
An 18thWall Productions book published by
arrangement with Nicole Petit
verba mea in minibus
desiderium meum
Cover by Morgan Fitzsimons
Design by Elisgraphics
Text Copyright
The Dragon Lord's Secretary © 2016 Nicole Petit
The Magic Realm Manuscripts and all related characters © Nicole Petit

To my Parents
For their Patience and Dedication

Table of Contents

Chapter 1

Deep in the land where magic hides, in the court of the Dragon Lord, a war as old as Camelot raged. Down past the caverns carved by dwarven hands, laced with streams of gold, fire blazed and armor clashed. Past the cavern halls smoke smudged the tableau. It seeped, black and riotous, from the mouths of slain guards. Roars shook the roots of the mountain.

In the throne room, a Knight brandished his shield against the mighty Dragon Lord.

Gales of wind from great black wings beat against the small body of the Knight. A wave of his hand and the mighty winds turned, slamming with greater force against the dragon's great head. The beast snarled, unveiling rows of sharp teeth.

"SUCH MAGIC DOES NOT IMPRESS ME, CHILD OF THE WIND."

Each rumbling word beat the Knight's armor; the force of sound slammed against his ribs.

"That was no magic, lizard. That was a warning. I've killed two of your kind today. Release your captive and you won't be the third."

The Dragon Lord circled the Knight. "WARNINGS CARRY MORE WEIGHT WHEN YOU HOLD MORE THAN A SHIELD TO COWER BEHIND."

The golden blade attached to his whip-tail sliced through the shield and the power of its protective runes. The Knight howled, arm shattered by the force of the blow. The floor heaved beneath him as the dragon moved forward, each step causing tremors in the cave.

The jewel which hung around the Dragon Lord's neck flared through the smoke. The massive gem was said to contain the flame of the very first dragon, a power more ancient than the entirety of the Knight's own race. The Dragon Lord towered over the fallen Knight, opening his jaws wide to call forth the ancient flame buried deep in his chest.

CRACK!

A whip made of the wind sliced through the roof of the Dragon Lord's mouth. Blood quenched the fire. The Dragon Lord reared back from his prey.

"Weight only burdens you, lead scales."

Blood continued to choke the Dragon Lord, but the fury boiling in his molten gold eyes said enough. Gold claws shot toward the Knight's chest. The Knight pulled back his whip and…

"I swear I leave the room for one hour and the whole place goes to pot."

From the secret tunnels behind the Dragon's Throne a young lady appeared. Curls of strawberry blonde hair escaped the tight bun and bounced across a pair of black rimmed glasses. Eyes the tangly green of spanish moss peered over the rims of her glasses. With a steady rhythm she tapped a pen against a notepad resting in one arm. The Dragon Lord stepped forward, his bloodied mouth hanging open. She gasped, resting the pen against her lips.

"Lord Almighty!"

The dragon smiled, his voice almost a purr. "Yes, Miss Chase?"

"Not *you*. The *merciful* one. Come down here, let me see." She crooked a finger. The dragon lowered his head, resting it against the floor. One slitted pupil kept a close watch on the Knight. The lady leaned in between his teeth, peering up at the wound. As she prodded experimentally with her pen the dragon writhed and snarled.

The Knight brandished his whip, "Step back, m'lady. I'll set you free from this beast."

Miss Chase pulled back, making notes on her notepad. "Beast is a horrible slur. It would be proper to call the Great and Glorious Dragon Lord Calix by his name, which just so happens to be the Great and Glorious Dragon Lord Calix. What, exactly, makes you think I need to be freed?"

The Knight stepped forward, laying a hand on her shoulder. His voice softened. "You're his slave."

She grimaced at the creases his armor made against her green blouse. With distaste she brushed off his heavy hand.

"Slave? Sir, I'm his secretary."

Chapter 2

"And then you have a meeting with the Elder Wyrms For Wyvern Equality at three."

"LEVIATHAN BURN IT ALL! NOT THOSE WALKING CASES OF SCALE ROT."

Heaps of gold shuddered under the force of Calix's bellow. Priceless and highly breakable objects tumbled from their piles. The secretary sighed as she walked beside him, struggling to keep her hair in its bun as the wind whipped up by the Knight grew wilder and wilder.

"Would you mind taking this fight elsewhere? I *just* alphabetized the dwarven artifacts."

"PRIORITIES, MISS CHASE! MY KINGDOM IS IN PERIL!" A burst of flame scorched Calix's collection of Dragon-proof armor. He fled into the deeper reaches of the Dragon Lord's hoard. Calix chased after to be met with a crack of the whip against his muzzle. He roared, and a furious lash of his tail cast an entire pile of gold upward. A flick of the secretary's wrist and the gold hung in the air.

Miss Chase arched a brow. "Peril? A single mage?"

"YES, PERIL! YOU LET ONE PEST IN AND AN INFESTATION IS SURE TO FOLLOW." He leaned down close and cleared his throat. "This would all be much easier if you would just let me eat him."

Miss Chase lowered her hand, and the gold fell back into a neat pile. "Or, you know, I could just use my—"

"NO. I'M THE HOST, HE'S MY UNWANTED GUEST. I'LL DEAL WITH HIM, NOT YOU." With a lash of his wings the

Dragon Lord slid off, scattering treasures as he went. Miss Chase sighed and made herself as comfortable as she could in a particularly rickety golden throne. The cavern shuddered. Gales of wind knocked over her carefully arranged vases, and plumes of fire displaced her organization. Dabbing the tip of her finger against her tongue she flipped through the pages on her notepad.

"Make it quick, my lord. You have a board meeting in an hour."

"**BOARD MEETING? HELLHOUNDS TAKE YOU AND YOUR STRANGE PHRASEOLOGY, SECRETARY!**"

A furious roar, a scattering of gold, and the Knight was launched high into the air by a swat from Calix's claws. His tail twitched merrily, molten gold eyes glittering at the sight. Instead of the clatter of armor against floor Calix expected, he was met with a furious blast of magic. Not the wind he had come to expect, but a more dazzling sort of shockwave that could only come from...

Miss Chase yelped and rushed through the thin paths, stopping at the section she reserved for cursed items. She came to a shield of some long forgotten race (knocked woefully out of place) and stopped. It was metallic with a milky white gloss, and shaped like a chrysalis' wing. Much too delicate for its purpose. Miss Chase stared at it, tracing the thin lines with her eyes. These lines pulsed with a silver light that she never recalled being there before. Confronted with a strange new glow in the cursed items section of Calix's hoard, she did what any self-respecting secretary would. She tapped on it with her pen.

The shield quivered, the lights pulsed bright. "IN THE NAME OF ALL THE OLD GODS OF ATLANTIS,

WHERE AM I? WHAT HAVE YOU DONE TO ME, BEAST?"

Calix threw back his head and laughed, drowning out the Knight's cries. Miss Chase gave a resigned sigh, adding a note at the very bottom of her to-do list:

Free Knight from cursed treasure.

Chapter 3

"Already here, my lord."

"Secretary, come at once!"

He rumbled, goblets and crowns tumbling off his sleek muzzle.

"The polite thing to do, mage, is to wait until after I call for you to answer."

A lopsided smile snuck across her lips. She tapped the tip of her pen against her temple. "You did call. It was just veeeeery slooooooow getting from your head to your tongue. I was impatient."

A royal snort. "Do compose yourself."

She did. Calix sighed, a cloud of smoke puffed from his nostrils. It poured over the treasure, snaked toward Miss Chase and wrapped her in its heady cinnamon scent. He wormed deeper into the pile of gold and gems, stretching his long body. The enchanted shield that served as the Knight's prison bounced against his neck. The Knight had gone completely silent in the past few days, so naturally Calix decided he would make a good trophy necklace.

With a great sigh, he spoke. "Today I present my glory to the grown hatchlings."

Miss Chase cocked her head, "Never heard you bemoan revealin' your glory before." She took a note on her notepad. Calix buried himself in his treasure, grumbling about "throwing gold before magi." A flick of her wrist and that gold tumbled off him, leaving his tender scales exposed to the elements. "Well, if it's such a trial, let's end your suffering swiftly."

Calix caught her up in his tail and settled her between his wings. He set off with little ceremony—a cursory tip of the wings to his guards. He chuffed down the tunnels, where ancient dwarven runes were carved into veins of glowing ore. He climbed up through crystal caverns shaped by countless scrapes of claws. Light shown at the end of the cavern, and he spread his wings. Out of his mountain home he soared, climbing high past the peak. A sharp turn had Miss Chase scrambling for a hold, as well as giving her a beautiful view of the kingdom below.

North, beyond the mountains crowned by Leviathan's Peak, stretched the Cracked Lands, a harsh desert from the days when an overeager sun scorched the new world, and now only a home for exiles and wyverns. To the south stretched the more temperate plains of Calix's domain, and where newly founded mage-towns pushing against the dragons borders.

A quick twitch and Miss Chase was thrown from his back, plummeting to the ground far below. She yelped, mind sifting quickly through her options of spells.

Wings pulled tight to his body, Calix dove steep. He laughed, twisting around her, carving tunnels into the sparse clouds. As the ground came up to meet them, his mighty wings flared and he settled on the edge of a cavern not far from his throne in Leviathan's Peak.

He plucked his secretary out of the air with his tail and set her before him. She huffed, smoothed her blouse and skirt, and straightened her glasses.

Catching her breath she stated, "Rather roundabout route, really."

Calix thrummed, head bobbing. "Need to stretch the wings now and then. Come, secretary, let me welcome you to our nests."

Close to the earth, the caverns went down, down, down. The tunnels were more humble, raked out by sharp claws, rubbed smooth by scales. Not a glint of gold or glow of crystal. The deeper they delved, the warmer it grew. A layer of dragon's smoke covered the ground; it issued from many dragons from what Miss Chase could tell by the mix of scents, each unique smoke belonging to an individual below. The heady scents began to overwhelm.

"Good Lord, it's like being in a candle store." She snapped her fingers and summoned a kerchief, tying it around her face.

Calix's scales bristled at the remark. "Enough of your strange words and insults, secretary. It's unwise to upset a nesting mother."

She cleared her throat. "Terr'bly sorry, sir. Your, er, incense is a bit too much for my shamefully inadequate schnoz."

Calix turned a golden eye on her. "You should come with a dictionary."

The tunnel gave way to hot springs. The dragon's nests were set as close to the warmth as manageable. The lanky lungs wrapped around their eggs, whiskers prickling and coils tightening as the secretary passed. They were larger and longer than Calix, and a mane of soft fur ran down their back. The lungs had no wings, but Miss Chase had come to recognize the tell-tale *swoosh* of one climbing through the sky like a snake through water.

Cohuatls perched on their high nests, eyeing the

stranger. They were tubby winged snakes with stubby viper noses and spikey scales mixed with brilliant plumage. The cohuatls took a great deal of pride in the fact that they more closely resembled the mother of dragons, Aida the Rainbow Serpent, than the rest of their kind.

Calix and the rest of his kin were content to call themselves, simply, dragons. They came in a much wider variety of size and shape than the more pedigreed lungs and cohuatls. Some had great crests of horns, others delicate frills. There were thick builds, and heavy plates of scales, and willowy sylphs who were nearly transparent.

Miss Chase sensed no hostility from the mothers, but there was no love lost here. She jotted down notes, unfazed. This was the typical reaction to her presence from any dragon who was not her boss. It was the hatchlings, too young to have left the nest, who bounded forward without a hint of reservation.

"Wow! A mage! Mother was right, Lord Calix does keep a pet."

Miss Chase crinkled her nose and peered over her glasses. "I'm no pet, I'm an employee."

The hatchlings blundered on.

"Look at how it walks! Two legs!" cried a lung. She tried to copy the mage's walk, but tied herself in knots.

A cohuatl too young to fly slithered over, perching on her shoulders. "It's so small, I wonder how big they get!"

Another dragon tangled himself in her legs. "I've heard they can spit water from their mouths!"

Miss Chase laughed. With more flourish than necessary she summoned an item none of the dragons had ever seen. Though the soft glint of bronze was enough to interest even the most cool eye. "Now y'all watch this, I'm a champion spitter. I'll land it right in that spittoon yonder."

True to her word, the secretary shot an impressive spitball into the spittoon with a satisfying *ding!* The hatchlings crooned, staring up at her in awe. She stuck out her tongue for further inspection.

The cohuatl hatchling prodded experimentally with the tip of his tail then chirped, "Wet! Water! Oh no wonder the wyverns traded their fire—"

The adults hissed at the name of their sworn enemy, and the hatchlings cowered. Before Miss Chase had time to intervene, the largest hot spring bubbled violently. From the depths burst a long neck and massive head, nearly three times the size of the Dragon Lord. Her smooth scales were dark as midnight, but with a rainbow sheen enhanced by the steam and water. She shared a crest of horns with the Dragon Lord, though hers were greater in number than the three on either side of Calix's head, as well as naturally dark without the ornaments of gold. Her eyes, though milky white, were sharp and searching. The nesting mothers all bowed low, murmuring respects to the "Great Wyrm."

"**OH! MY DARLING SON HAS COME TO VISIT, HOW LOVELY! COME HERE, SWEET CHILD. LET ME SEE HOW MUCH YOU'VE GROWN. OH YOU ARE SUCH A HANDSOME YOUNG DRAKE,**" she crooned, her high voice booming.

The great Dragon Lord Calix shuffled his claws and burbled. Miss Chase rested her hands on her hips, "Now hold on, I've been with you for three years and never once have you brought me home to mother?"

The Great Wyrm bobbed her head, the dragon's version of a smile. "**AND YOU MUST BE THE MAGE I HAVE HEARD**

SO MUCH OF, THE NEW PET OF CALIX. HOW DARLING!
YOU EVEN GOT YOURSELF ONE OF THE SPECKLED ONES,
CALIX. WHAT MAGIC DOES THIS ONE WIELD? THEY SAY
SHE IS A SECRETARY. I HAVE NOT HEARD OF SUCH A
SPECIALTY."

Now that attention turned off him, Calix regained his composure. He wound his neck around Miss Chase and looked her over. "Speckled? Hmmm. I thought they were blemishes." One of the hatchlings ventured near him and reached out to prod his tail. He grunted and swatted them away.

Miss Chase adjusted her glasses and assumed an air of professionalism. "Ahem. They're freckles. Secretary, not pet, is my title. Empath is my specialty."

The Great Wyrm took this all in, head bobbing along. "OH HOW NICE. IT HAS BEEN HUNDREDS OF YEARS SINCE I'VE HAD THE PLEASURE OF A MAGE'S COMPANY, THOUSANDS SINCE ONE WAS AN EMPATH. SUCH A RARE TALENT FOR YOUR KIND. LAST ONE I KNEW GOT LOST IN A CAVE SOMEWHERE. I WONDER WHAT HAPPENED TO HIM. HMM, THIS WAR BETWEEN US DOES PUT A DAMPER ON RELATIONS, COLD AS IT MAY BE. TELL ME, DEAR, WHAT IS YOUR NAME?"

"Scarlet, Mrs.—er—Wyrm. Pleased to meetcha."

Calix thrummed at this. "Scarlet? I thought you were Miss Chase."

His secretary arched a brow. "Miss *Scarlet* Chase, to be exact."

Calix growled. "You never told me your name was Scarlet."

"Three years and you never bothered to ask. Or read my

resume."

Two hatchlings gathered the courage to approach the Dragon Lord, distracting him from the conversation. A warning growl sent them scurrying away.

The Wyrm thrummed. "I DON'T BLAME YOU, DEAR, FOR MISSING THE ELDER WYRMS FOR WYVERN EQUALITY MEETING WHEN YOU HAVE SUCH A LOVELY LITTLE COMPANION."

Scarlet's eyes widened. "Waitwaitwait. You're one of the 'walking cases of scale rot'?"

"OH IS THAT WHAT WE'RE CALLED THESE DAYS?" She thrummed, almost a chuckle. "YES, LITTLE ONE, I'M THE HEAD OF IT!"

Scarlet threw back her head and laughed. She smacked Calix's snout. "You never told me your *mom* was a part of this."

A crowd of the hatchlings wound their way between Calix's legs. His fangs came down like guillotines, and his tail lashed. He whirled around, wreathing himself in smoke and flame. He reared up, wings flared wide, and the first embers of dragonfire kindled. The hatchlings froze, curling tails tight around themselves. He roared, and what followed shook the mountain's roots.

"YOU THINK YOU ARE TO BE CONGRATULATED? YOU THINK YOU ARE DRAGONS?" He curled his claws into the rock and it came up as dust. "YOU ARE MERE LIZARDS. NO FLIGHT, NO FIRE, UNWORTHY OF MY NOTICE."

Scarlet recoiled, clutching at her head.

The Great Wyrm chuffed. "NOW THAT'S NOT VERY KIND OF YOU, CALIX. SCARING THE HATCHLINGS, GIVING YOUR EMPATH A HEADACHE. THEY'RE ALL VERY

SENSITIVE, YOU KNOW."

The rest of the squabble was lost on Scarlet, her mind seared by the Dragon Lord's sudden rage. She stumbled back, dazed, tripped on a dragon's claw and fell down onto its foot. The nesting mother lashed her tail and batted Scarlet away. Scarlet's glasses fell, a lens popped out and cracked. The dragons not involved with Calix's display turned to watch. Scarlet brushed herself off and held up her hands.

"It's okay, I don't need 'em anyway. I just use those to look smart."

"Your kind is the reason mine are so small in number. Your kind pushes against our borders. We are at war with you. Why our Lord keeps you here I do not know—"

"To be fair, it's a cold war. You stopped burning towns and they stopped building more. You stopped kidnapping nobles and knights stopped coming to take 'em back. Y'all just kinda glare at each other from a distance, and sometimes you eat their sheep. And me, well, the big fella keeps me because I can type a solid eighty-five words per minute, no mistakes. I'm not even slowed by the typewriter's carriage bar because magic—"

"Go back to your towns and burn." Flames licked the edges of her fangs, neck arched back in preparation to strike.

Scarlet arched a brow. "Now, that's just rude."

A flash of midnight scales wrapped in bronze. Aurum had come. Radiant Raider of the Cracked Lands, Herald of the Dragon Lord. She pounced on the nesting mother, wrapping her lithe body around the larger dragon. The nesting mother bellowed as Aurum's needle claws dug into the spots where scales did not protect. She didn't roar; she hissed through a snarl. "You dare slight the great Lord of Dragons in his very presence? I should kill you now."

Calix grew quiet and turned toward his Herald. Aurum's words caused the other dragons to shudder.

The Great Wyrm chuffed. "**DEATH IS A HEFTY PRICE, AURUM, FOR HER AND US. WE ARE SO FEW IN NUMBER NOW, AND OUR CLUTCHES SMALL. I TAUGHT YOU, AND ALL HERE, NOT TO KILL YOUR OWN KIND.**"

Aurum tightened her coils. "You taught me our laws. You know that such a slight against the reigning lord is a killing offense."

Scarlet dashed forward. "Woah, woah, hold on. She didn't insult him, it was me she was after. No need to throw the death penalty around now."

Aurum snorted. "You belong to the Dragon Lord. To slight you is to affront him. But you're right, you mean little in the great scheme of things. I shall show mercy and rip her wings off instead."

The mother writhed. "No, please! Don't bring such shame on my house. I would rather you kill me swiftly."

A shudder passed through the stumps where Aurum's wings should have been. Her eyes narrowed. "I bear the shame just fine, wretch. And so will you." She opened her jaws wide, arched her neck high, and...

Twitched.

Her bronze eyes turned toward Scarlet. "I feel you in my mind, mage," she spat. "Release your hold on me now. Let me do my job."

The secretary's face had hardened, nearly a match for the Radiant Raider. "No. I can't let you do that. It's not right."

Aurum hissed. "Calix, you let this mage speak too freely. Shut her mouth."

Calix kept silent and still, eyes half lidded, face inscrutable.

It was the Great Wyrm who intervened. "**AURUM, MY CHILD, PLEASE. STEP DOWN.**"

Scarlet released her hold on Aurum's mind. The raider loosed her coils and slithered toward Calix's side. She looked him over and chuffed. "It's not wise, Lord, to let a mage speak for you. It casts a bad image to your subjects. Some might think you grow too attached to her."

Calix didn't bother to glance her way. "She does not speak for me, Raider. Neither do you."

Aurum's crest of spines bristled, she snapped her fangs but held her tongue.

Calix turned to his secretary. "Aurum, my right wing, my sister, has a right to dispense justice in my name. You dared to stand in her way because you claim this isn't right. Well then, mage, since you certainly know best—" he chuffed "—what do you propose we do?"

Scarlet swallowed. All eyes were on her now. The nesting mother towered over her small form, waiting. Scarlet sighed. "Well, I guess we can't just let bygones be bygones." A negative rumble from the crowd confirmed that. "Alright then, uh, I heard about a time when the clever Aida punished a boastful Leviathan by binding his mouth."

Scarlet made a gesture much like tying a knot. The nesting mother jerked back and flared her wings, but her jaw stayed shut. Scarlet turned toward Calix, bowing. "Erm, if that's all pleasing to you, my lord."

22

Calix thrummed. "It would be unwise to refuse the wisdom of the first dragons, Miss...Scarlet." He rose, flaring his wings and arching his neck. "My secretary will free you in a week's time—by then I'll hope you'll have learned the benefits of a closed mouth." He snapped his jaws, a burst of flame licking his fangs.

He turned and headed toward the exit. "Come, secretary, I've spent enough time here as it is."

As Scarlet hurried to keep up with him, she heard the Great Wyrm call, "**WHEN YOU RETURN, CALIX, I'LL HAVE SOME WORDS WITH YOU ABOUT THE PROPER SPEECH TO GIVE A HATCHLING.**"

Calix growled and lashed his tail, ducking into the caverns. When they were safely out of range, he slowed and allowed his secretary to take her place at his side. He lowered his head to her level as he wormed along, studying her with one golden eye. "I was mistaken to think three years was enough to uncover all the secrets of a mage, Miss Scarlet."

Her lips twitched. "A first name and fake glasses, I'm just full of surprises."

Calix might have retorted if the shield around his neck hadn't interrupted. It rattled. The silver light pulsed. From within, the Knight spoke.

"It won't be our towns burning when the Firetail comes."

Calix chuffed and swatted at the shield. "Rather delayed comeback, Child of Wind." He looked back up to find Scarlet frozen, eyes wide and face pale.

Chapter 4

Dragons are sticklers for tradition, whether it be kidnapping royalty and eating knights, or rising in the early morning to catch the first rays of sun on their scales. Scarlet was never fond of the repetition of routine, but over the years she had learned to appreciate it.

Traditions are easy to exploit.

As the reptiles pulled themselves out of their caves, Scarlet slithered through the shadows in the other direction. While the dragons fought over their ancestral roosts on Aida's Watch, Scarlet slipped toward the sulphur lakes of Aikon's Flight.

Rock columns jutted up the face of Leviathan's Peak. Great pillars, again, and again, and again. Great steps had been carved into the cliff face. The highest step, so far above, was Aida's Watch. The second step was a name Scarlet couldn't recall, though she was sure it was Some Great Dragon's Thing. Now she slipped subtly down to the first step, into the canyon known as Aikon's Flight.

Her hand traced the patterns of the painted canyon walls, caressing each color with the familiar intimacy of an old lover.

The dragons say the winding canyon was formed by Aikon, father of Basilisks, as he fled from Leviathan. The beautiful scales that were the basilisk's glory rubbed off on the rocks as he passed, but his malice was also transferred. Geysers spewed boiling water that could melt the thick scales of dragonhide. One slip on the treacherous pass or rip in the wing could send a traveler plummeting into the white rapids of the river below. Only the most skilled, or stupid, of dragons dared follow the flight of the first basilisk. Which meant, Scarlet noted, that she was entirely alone.

Arm over arm she pulled herself up the cliff face, dodging the hissing geysers and crumbling rocks. She found a spot far enough away from the colorful, bubbling lakes, with a view of the dragons of Aida's Watch. She pulled her legs to her chest and rested her chin on her knees.

"Firetail."

The morning sun hovered above the dragons, stroking their scales with warm rays of light. Some of the hatchlings played at the edge, testing each other's mettle. With one lazy whip of the tail, an adult pushed them off the plateau. Scarlet's head snapped up. Even from this distance their fear pierced her mind. Tiny claws scraped at the rushing air. Wings flapped uselessly. Screeches ripped from their throats before they could make it to the adults above.

A rush of warm air filled their leather wings, pushing them up and away from the hungry earth. The hatchlings stopped flapping, instincts kicking in as they began to soar. Fear melted beneath wild ecstasy. A flash of scales and wings. The adult who had knocked them off now dove beneath them, not even a flap of her wings disturbing their flight. Gentle nudges from her broad snout lifted the young dragons higher and higher into the air. Squeals of delight came from the hatchlings when they finally ascended to the safety of Aida's Watch.

A shadow fell over their small bodies.

The Dragon Lord, wreathed in smoke and flame, appeared before the hatchlings. They shrunk from his mighty form. He lowered his head.

"REMEMBER WHEN I CALLED YOU LIZARDS, UNWORTHY OF MY NOTICE?" he rumbled, each word releasing a new tongue of fire.

The hatchlings froze, staring deep into his molten gold eyes.

The flames died, and the smoke faded. "NOW YOU ARE DRAGONS."

Aida's Watch erupted with the song of dragons. The hatchlings launched themselves at their lord, nuzzling against his muzzle. Calix grimaced and squirmed, but allowed the injustice. Many of the adults took to the air, twirling and weaving delicate patterns. They danced with their own twisting fire.

Scarlet smiled, shaking her head. The culture of fire-breathing reptiles never ceased to amaze her. She turned from the celebration, attention caught by a lone figure in flight. Far from the dragons, toward the Cracked Lands of the desert, a black speck shot through the sky. There was a fearful art in the grace and speed of the wings, slicing through the arid sky. It was a sharp contrast to the dance of the dragons, meant to dazzle with skill and flourish. This creature's movements were spartan, the product of desperate hunts and all the more desperate escapes.

The black speck grew larger, shooting past the colorful sulphur lakes and the painted geysers that made them. Black gave way to bronze. It was close enough that Scarlet could see the glint of the sun off scales. Closer still, she saw the onyx talons. It was nearly on top of her, and she saw the slitted pupils frosted in blue. The creature folded its leathery wings and dove, short jaw opened wide.

Panic is reserved for the dead. Scarlet jumped back, and the creature slammed against the parched ground. A screech rent the air, slicing through the dragon song. Scarlet locked eyes with the creature. Her hand raised; time seemed to slow.

The wyvern.

Ancient foe of the dragons. All of their animal rage and none of their sentiment. Scarlet's mind was seared by the wyvern's radiating hatred. She sensed the lunge before it happened, giving her more than enough time to dodge. Again and again the pattern repeated. A lash of the tail. A gorge of the horn. A snap of the jaw. Scarlet dodged, each time with a little less room to maneuver. Each time gave her a little more insight into the creature's mind. The clashing cymbals of rage hid a subtle melody, one weaved by more cunning than a mere beast was capable of.

But not more than hers.

The geysers of the sulphur lakes shuddered and hissed as they drew near. Boiling water erupted from their mouths, searing both mage and wyvern. She shrugged off the sting and drew it closer to the lakes, tendrils of her mind wrapping around the wyvern's.

It opened its mouth. Instead of the fire she anticipated, she got a face full of frost shards.

She staggered back.

Invading one's mind opens the door both ways. The wyvern sensed her shock. Did it smile? One wing opened, revealing a set of talons. Their tips sped toward her stomach.

Scarlet smiled back.

Boiling water from the now near geyser rent the leather wing. As the wyvern screeched and withdrew, Scarlet pulled away from the danger of the geysers. The land was an alien world to the wyvern, who was used to the open sky. It writhed, chasing after its prey. Pain rent the subtle melody Scarlet had heard in the wyvern's mind. It took a running leap, aiming both taloned feet at her small body.

Scarlet sighed.

One last dodge and the wyvern fell into the canyon, pulled beneath the white rapids. Scarlet fell to the ground. As the wyvern's mind was ripped from hers she was able to translate one final thought.

Trespasser.

The canyon erupted with screeches as three more wyverns rose to avenge their kin. They circled above. She hesitated, grabbing onto each mind, sifting quickly through alien thoughts. One opened its mouth; she dodged the bolt of lightning. Another opened; a flick of her wrist and a rock leapt up to block the spewing acid. The third never got the chance.

Bursts of brilliant flame burned holes in the creature's thin wings. It fell into the rapids like the first. Calix held Aurum in his claws. His massive shadow fell over the two remaining wyverns. The Dragon Lord let loose his grip on Aurum. She dove, landing on the back of another. They plummeted. The wyvern landed in the sulphur lake, scales seared by the boiling waters. Aurum slipped off his writhing body, stretching out on the sands and stifling a yawn. She watched Calix catch up the third in his claws, and crush it as he landed.

Scarlet polished her nails on her blouse. "Couldn't have come a little earlier, hero?"

Calix stepped off the wyvern and lounged. "I wanted to see what you were made of. If you had needed me earlier, I'd have come."

Aurum huffed. "Besides, it was your own fault. Only idiots come alone into Aikon's Flight. Suicidal trespassers, or—"

Calix rumbled, tail twitching happily. "Or very brave dragons."

"Of all the beautiful roosts to spend your morning on, why do you choose the deadliest place of all my kingdom?"

"Well, I used to pick it because it was secluded. You're getting in the way of that."

Scarlet leaned against the reclining Dragon Lord's leg. She filed her nails with studious care. Calix huffed, but felt no inclination to move. Absently he studied the dragons of Aida's Watch. The hatchlings now practiced soaring on the currents, with the adults keeping careful watch from beneath.

"Merely ensuring the safety of my secretary. Couldn't afford to train another one."

Scarlet tested the sharpened tips of her nails. She smiled. A snap of her fingers and a box landed neatly in her lap. She pulled out a flat, circular container the size of her palm. Pressing an indention in the bottom it revealed a mirror and a puff of cotton.

"Mind moving?" Scarlet asked, "Your ample girth is blocking the sun. Which I need for this *delicate* operation."

Any other day Calix might have threatened to eat her for

such impertinence. She was growing too comfortable in his presence. However, she did slay a wyvern. With only a low growl he complied. Scarlet gave him a wink.

Much too comfortable.

He glared at the back of her head, using the opportunity to learn about her mysterious new tools. Between the tips of her nails she pulled out the cotton and used it to dab dirt from the container onto her face. Scarlet didn't turn, but he could just feel her smile. "Remember that thing I said about coming here to be alone?"

"What in the sun's blazes are you doing to your face?"

She favored him with a lopsided grin. "Make-up. All the rage where I come from, sugah." Her voice dipped into a thicker accent, laced in a sugar sweet drawl. Closing the container she pulled out another. Using a stick she painted some lighter dirt on her eyelids. And then, another stick, used to paint lines around the edges of her eyes. Calix inched closer. He gave a curious thrum. She watched him from the corner of her eye.

This time she pulled out a cylinder, screwing off the top to reveal a funny little brush. She turned her back to him. As she caked mud on her eyelashes she opened her mouth slightly and stuck her tongue out the side of her mouth. Calix would have mocked her had he not realized that he had done it himself.

"Explain those words: Make. Up."

Scarlet giggled, pulling out another cylinder filled with pale pink clay and traced it over her mouth. Capping it, she made a popping sound with her lips.

"Ladies, aaand *occasional* gentlemen, use it to make their face look prettier. Nicer. Something like that."

Calix narrowed his eyes. "Does all that mud and dirt work?"

Scarlet arched a brow. "Seems to. I get a lot nicer smiles from boys this way. Why, do you oppose us hiding our true forms under a mask of carefully crafted subterfuge?"

"*Nooooo.*" Calix drew out the word. "If your own race finds you unattractive, this make-up does the world a favor." He paused, leaning toward Scarlet confidentially. "Though, if I may, I suggest you use a little more. Your blemishes still show."

Chapter 5

The cavern shuddered under the force of the Dragon Lord's roar. Smoke and fire poured from every tunnel as he stalked the shadows of his golden hoard. In the middle of it all a chair hovered over the sea of gold, jewels, and other, breakable objects. Scarlet polished the cursed shield, ignoring the raging reptile.

"**WHERE IS MY GOBLET! I KNOW YOUR WAYS, CHICANEROUS HELLHOUND, YOU STOLE IT WHILE I SLEPT!**"

Scarlet glanced up from her polishing. "Steal? I did exactly what you ordered me to—I cleaned up the Endless Hoard of the Great and Glorious Dragon Lord. I don't even *want* any of your dad-blamed treasure, you—you Lard Lizard!"

Calix reared up, his snarling fangs level with Scarlet's chair. "**RETURN MY TREASURE AND I WILL FORGET THAT SLIGHT, BLEMISHED MAGE IN NEED OF MUCH MAKE-UP.**"

Scarlet narrowed her eyes and scrunched her freckled face. "It's with the rest of the goblets, in the section specifically for shiny dinnerware, *oh great and glorious lord of all fire breathing reptiles.*" She gestured in that direction. Calix growled and slithered to the dinnerware section of his hoard. Burbling to himself, claws needling the rock, he sifted through the countless objects.

"I gave you very specific instructions. I told you to clean my hoard, not the treasure that is my throne. Now that you've organized it all, I'll never be able to find any of it ever again. **I WANTED TO RUB MY FACE AGAINST IT, YOU HEARTLESS WENCH!**"

"THEY'RE SORTED AND ALPHABETIZED BY COLOR, CLOD!"

The cursed shield shuddered in her hands. "If you do not free me, Firetail will burn your mountain to its roots—"

Calix turned at the sound of the Knight.

Scarlet yowled and hurled it across the cavern, beaming him. He yelped and flopped over, rubbing at his face with his front claws. Scarlet gasped and covered her mouth. The chair dropped to the floor. She jumped up and rushed over to the writhing Dragon Lord.

"Sorrysorrysorry." She crooned and patted his muzzle.

Calix's tail lashed, scattering goblets everywhere. **"STAY BACK! YOU HAVE THE SENSIBILITIES OF A WYVERN."**

"Awww Calix I'm sorry I really am I didn't mean it." She turned to the goblet section, rummaging through the wreckage. "Look! Here! See, here's your goblet, polished and ready to be nuzzled."

Calix lowered a claw from his eyes, thrumming. But he didn't take the goblet.

Scarlet frowned. "What can I do to make this better?"

The dragon continued to thrum, claws sliding slowly off his muzzle. "Tell me about this Firetail who bothers you so." His lips pulled up in a gesture unnatural to dragons. A smile. A grin to be precise, one he had learned from studying her. Scarlet's expression went stony, the spark in her grey-green eyes dulled.

"Dragons hoard everything, especially knowledge. You don't give that for free. Why should I?"

Calix kept his grin, scooting closer and bumping his muzzle against her. "But we do *trade*."

Scarlet hesitated. She rested her elbows on his muzzle and her chin on her palms. She studied him closely through squinted eyes. "And what, exactly, do you have to offer?"

"I see you know our lore. It interests you, doesn't it?"

"I know some, yeah. My brothers are librarians back in the mage's capitol, I know what little they do, and I know whatever I've been able to glean around you. You have interesting stories."

Calix crooned and grinned wider. A bump of his snout guided her in the direction of a tunnel that had before now been forbidden to her. "Come then, Scarlet, I believe I have some knowledge worth trading."

Scarlet grunted and allowed him to herd her along, his excitement so tangible she could sense it without even trying. "How much do you know about dragon hoards, Scarlet?"

"Uh, y'all like shiny things."

"Yes, yes, that's universal. What about *individual* hoards?"

"Like opinions, everyone has one. Some are better than others."

The melody of his mind burst into vibrant color, she didn't just sense his glee now, she saw it. "First trade, you can tell much about a dragon by their hoard. Not the shiny one. The secret one. The one that holds their most treasured...erm...treasure."

"That's not good enough to tell you about Firetail, Calix."

"Does it get me something about you?"

34

"One of those secrets it's taken you three years to uncover? Sure. My brothers are older than me, so is my sister. She's the oldest. I'm the youngest. She's a well-respected mage. *Very* well-respected. Like, Hosting-Parties-For-Magi-High-Council-Respected."

"Are you?"

Scarlet clamped her mouth shut.

Another bump of Calix's snout and Scarlet found herself in a new cavern. It was smaller than the rest, filled with shelves upon shelves of books and scrolls. Calix bounced eagerly, watching for her reaction. "This is my private hoard."

Scarlet cast a glance around. "Hm. Yeah. Does say a lot about you. Most dragons like reading even less than I do."

Calix burbled. "You don't like reading?"

"Yep. There's your trade. What else you got?"

Calix grumbled, "One of the few things I like about your race is your reverence of knowledge."

Scarlet grinned and tapped the side of her head. "I like knowledge. Don't like books. I read minds, much more interesting. Next?"

Calix wrapped Scarlet up in his tail and wormed through his bookshelves, puffing smoke as he went. "Books *are* knowledge, mage. Dragons once had Lorekeepers, recorders of such knowledge. My ancestors belong to that caste. Highly revered once. Not so much now, in the age of war."

"That's cause y'all can't see in people's heads. You write thoughts down to make people privy to 'em. I prefer the direct method. I'll trade you this, though, I could shut that dragon's mouth only because she wasn't expecting it. I didn't have to fight her will. I can only really read people who are open or unaware. I have a few tricks up my sleeve, though, to worm my way in."

Calix rumbled, something like a chuckle. "Now that is a good trade."

"*Very* well."

"How well do you read mine—oh. Now...what in here would get you to trade about the Firetail."

"That's the name of the game right there."

"Hmmmmm. You like Leviathan and Aida. Perhaps more about them?"

"Maaaaaaaaybe."

He delicately plucked a leather bound tome from its shelf—it much too small for a dragon's claws—and he hobbled to a nook in the back he hollowed out for reading, careful not to let the claw with the book touch the ground. He curled up and plopped Scarlet between his front legs. He lifted the book up with his tail to his eyes, and squinted at the text. "This would be easier if you liked reading, secretary."

Scarlet chuckled. "It's what you get for choosing a hobby definitely not designed for dragons. How *did* your Lorekeepers manage?"

"These are dwarven translations. Lorekeepers kept such things verbally, and carved in cavern walls dedicated to that hallowed purpose. The caverns have since been lost and forgotten. It took me many years to even find these translations. What does that trade gain me?"

"Hmmmm." She grew quiet. This was the first to require thought. His wings bristled, he knew he was getting closer. "Knowing where the caverns are would've net you all about me and Firetail easy. I would love to see 'em. It's kinda cute, thinking about you snuffling up these books like a pig for truffles though. Well, I'm not full mage. My mother was mortal. Not-from-the-magic-realm kind of mortal. That's where I get my 'phraseology.' And where secretaries come from."

Calix thrummed. "I suspected. Yet, few travel to the mortal realm since Camelot. I know of no mage willing to risk death for that kind of adventure."

"More than you think, but less than a lot."

"That is vague and unhelpful, secretary."

"It wasn't a part of the trade, lard lizard."

Calix flipped through pages with the tip of his tail. "Hmmm. You know how Leviathan was forged from starfire and placed in the sea to cool. Aida was forged from cooler starfire and placed in the sky. Correct?"

Scarlet lounged against his leg. "Yep, yep. Got all that."

"Do you know how they died?"

"They died? Well. Yeah I guess they would have. Or else I'd see them around sometimes. No, I don't know how."

"Neither does anyone else."

"That's a flake trade."

"There is a legend, though, about the place *where* they died. It's far out in the Cracked Lands. Far past Aikon's Flight and the wyvern's territory, there is a great city built from the bones of the very first dragons. A city of refuge for the exiles, those seeking new lives. A city for thieves to retire and murderers to hide. The outcasts go there, and die there. Perhaps this trade…"

"Friesian. General Friesian. A centaur in the magi army.

37

He killed people I cared for. I won't let that happen again."

Scarlet grew silent, eyes locked on the floor, lips set in a hard line. Calix lowered his head to her side.

"Is that all you'll tell me?"

Scarlet stood up and headed for the cavern exit. "Find out how Leviathan and Aida died. Then you'll get the rest."

Chapter 6

"**M**ISS **S**CARLET **C**HASE."

The Dragon Lord's bellows shook the foundations of the mountain. There was a second's pause. Then he felt the gossamer strings drape over the edges of his mind, in a way that was once too subtle for him to notice. He didn't bother to turn and ruin his majestic pose. Calix growled. "Late."

"Long distance call you had there. You yelled so loud I could hear you in the mortal realm. Took a minute for me to respond. Had I been closer, I would've been here before you called, right on time."

He craned his neck to find her in a strange outfit. Thick helmet resting on her head, colored brightly. Pads everywhere. On her feet, shoes with wheels. He rumbled impatiently. "I wouldn't have needed to call 'long distance' you if stayed in the magic realm like a proper mage."

"Wouldn't leave if there was a decent derby league here." She huffed, then added, "Why're you complainin' anyway? Today was my day off!"

"I never gave you a day off!"

"It's in my contract, you big clod, the one I wrote up when you hired me. I get weekends off. You never read it did you? No wonder you never pay me!"

"Pay you?" Calix roared. "For centuries I've kidnapped royalty and never once did they demand pay!"

"You didn't kidnap me, dope! You hired me! Here, have a look!" She summoned her contract and chucked it at his nose.

Calix snorted and rubbed his snout. He picked the contract up and inspected it. After a moment of squinting and burbling about illegible mage swirls he tossed it over his shoulder, curled up and covered himself with smoke.

Scarlet rolled back and forth on her wheels. She sucked in a breath, and spoke in a more measured tone. "This what you called me here for? Some kind of smoke break?" The smoke pulled back from the reclining Dragon Lord, his tail flicking back and forth with the absent precision of a metronome.

"No, no, not quite. How do you say it, Scarlet? Close, but not charred?"

"No cigar, my lord. Close, but no cigar."

Calix snorted, releasing another puff of cinnamon smoke. "I prefer mine." Turning his attention back to Leviathan's Fire, he rapped a gold sheathed claw against the powerful gem. It glowed softly, the old magic stirring at his call. "I found an interesting tale in my library. It tells of the Chicanerous and Cunning Lord Aryx. He was small, pitifully weak. However, never outmatched for cleverness. He could not harness the fire of Leviathan to burn the cities of the enemy. Instead he harnessed the shifting smoke also held within the gem. It is said he could disguise himself as his foes, infiltrating their cities and destroying them from within."

Scarlet dodged a particularly enthusiastic whip of his tail. "Well the former Dragon Lord sounds like a swell guy. Is there a particular reason you wanted me to hear this story?"

"I'm trying to master the ability. Brute force is becoming less and less useful in this day and age," Calix answered. He lowered his head, inspecting his secretary with one eye. "Hm. Perhaps I should try your form first. I am most familiar with it. With practice I might be able to remove the blemishes and add some muscle."

Scarlet narrowed her eyes. "It'd be an improvement on the current you."

The Dragon Lord gave a warning rumble. Leviathan's Fire gleamed. Smoke poured from between his teeth, covering his body. Scarlet rolled a few steps back. The smoke cleared, leaving no sight of the Dragon Lord. In his place stood a man. Dark, smooth skin cloaked in a sunset red robe. He grunted, inspecting himself as if for the first time.

From his mouth slipped a familiar silky tone, "Hm. Unexpected." He rolled the words over his tongue. "How do I look, Miss Chase?"

"You look with your eyes, sir."

There was a pause. Calix studied her face but found it as hard to read as it always was. Then, slowly, Calix forced out an awkward laugh. "This is laughing, yes? Your joke is splendid."

Scarlet arched a brow. "Oh Lord, you're gonna need some practice before you blend in. Not some. A lot."

Calix swung his arms about, testing his new limbs. "Yes, if only there was a safe place to study the ways of bipeds without danger of being caught."

Scarlet smiled wide. "I have the perfect place."

That day Calix learned how the magi were able to teleport, and why they couldn't do so within Leviathan's Peak. Leylines, Scarlet called them. They hovered in the air, invisible to all except the children forged from the wind. Scarlet, being such a mage, could take a hold and use them to travel to any other leyline as long as she knew where she wanted to go. There were no leylines in Leviathan's Peak or the Cracked Lands beyond. So she took him to just such a place nestled in the plains between the Peak and the encroaching mage towns.

She took him by the hand, reached up to tug some invisible string. There was a sound like tearing fabric and they appeared in a strange, open-roofed tunnel. He growled, the sound not nearly as threatening when coming from mammal lips. Scarlet paid him no mind, picking at her derby outfit. A quick snap of her fingers and she gained a new one. It was bright and sunny, with less fabric than typical mage fare. "Last time I was here, Annette Funicello was wearing something like this."

Before Calix had time to ask, another snap of her fingers and he gained what she called a suit. Calix had never seen his secretary so excited. Granted, he had never seen her so close either. She was small before but now, well, she was a little less so.

"Now we can blend in nicely," she said. He grinned, grabbing her wrist and pulling her toward the entrance.

A strange sun glinted off more metal than that of a dwarven forge. Roars and bellows from iron carriages rushing past. Splashes of color thrown against walls miles high. Mass of flesh and cloth pressed together tight. Grass? No. None for miles. No trees. No beasts. Just—

"Mortals. Not magi. Welcome to the mortal realm, year of *their* lord 1963."

Calix took it all in, he could feel Scarlet bouncing on her heels.

A slow smile spread across his face. "Let's explore." Scarlet gave a whoop as she took over.

"No need to wander, boss, I know exactly where to go."

The world seemed so much bigger on the ground. Calix had flown past cities twice the size of this New York that Scarlet knew so well. Yet he never once expected there to be so much life in one place. He wondered how his ancestor was capable of bringing it down from within.

Buildings gave way to boardwalks and beach. Scarlet sensed a change in the Dragon Lord's mood; she paused and looked up into his face. She was studying him. He could feel her flitting over the surface of his thoughts.

He cleared his throat. "It's been ages since I saw the sea up close. Your kind keeps us...*contained*...to the Cracked Lands."

For once, the retort he expected never came. Scarlet studied his face. "There has to be a way..." she trailed, diverting her gaze to the waves.

"A way?"

"To get a good hotdog around here! No. Not just good. Legendary. Calix, it's time to introduce you to the crowning glory of mortal civilization! A place so weird you'll fit right in, no problem." The speed at which she perked up nearly gave Calix whiplash. Before he could react he was drawn through a mighty arch, alien runes scrawled along the top.

Coney Island, the pinnacle of mortal enlightenment. Rows and rows of colorful booths as far as the eye could see dared the travelers to conquer their challenges, explore their mysteries, buy their food. To all of which Scarlet and Calix gladly obliged, tossing the hawkers coins of gold from Calix's hoard. The Dragon Lord didn't bother to haggle price, the hawkers didn't ask where he got it. The curiosity-quenching power of wealth transcended race and realm.

"This is the best of all worlds. Such a dragonish race that they speak Draconic."

"Naw. 'Til you get on your linguistic feet I'm filtering all auditory stuff through my head to yours. C'mon, let's ride that!"

After some careful scouting of the land from atop the Ferris Wheel, Calix discovered the thrill of the Roller Coaster. "A whole different world when you're not controlling the flight, ain't it?" Scarlet yelled over the rush of wind. Calix scrambled for a hand hold in the wooden car. The sharp turns and steep drops that Calix so easily performed with wings now tossed him about. As the car jerked to a precarious halt, her squeals melted into laughter. As she jabbed him in the side with her elbow he frowned. This world she claimed as her own was filled with power far beyond what her fragile body could ever hope to harness.

Why didn't it make her feel small?

Scarlet loved the Fun Houses. She would lose Calix in the labyrinth and listen as he loudly cursed the "magic mirrors." He could hear her cackle every time he sprung a trap on himself. At the end of his wits he raised a fist, prepared to smash his tortured image in the mirror. A small hand wrapped around his. Scarlet flashed him a lopsided smile. "Stop trying to scare inanimate objects into submission. You're not made of scales and lard anymore. You'd just hurt yourself." She led him through the maze, stopping on occasion to make faces in the twisted mirrors.

"What do you suggest I do instead?"

"Just sit back and enjoy the ride."

It took two hot dogs, a funnel cake, another roller coaster, and beating Scarlet at the Steeple Chase for Calix to fully understand what she meant.

"Of course you won." Scarlet stated as she stole some of his cotton candy. "It's based on weight. The ride was made specifically for you."

Calix smiled, pulling the pink sugar fluff out of her reach. "Now, now, don't get bent out of shape. The Fun House did that for you."

A gnarled hand shot out from a booth, latching onto Calix's arm. He halted, frowning. "Is touching a very big thing with mammals?"

Scarlet shrugged, turning to the old woman behind the booth. The light from a crystal ball traced old skin, thin and crinkled like coffee-stained paper. Glassy eyes held the same dull glint as the cracked jewel on her turban. "Such a strange couple. The fates must rest heavy on you."

"We're as much a couple as you are a psychic," Scarlet grumbled, snatching some more cotton candy.

Calix drew closer, and the old woman released her grip. "Tell me what fates rest on us, child of wind."

"She's not..."

The old woman held out her hand, a gesture Calix had grown to understand as a request for payment. Shoving the cotton candy at an all too eager Scarlet, he pulled out a gold coin and placed it in the psychic's palm. Smoke poured from the crystal ball as she stared into its depths. "Ahh, you come from a far off land. Unused to our customs and culture, this young lady has become your guide."

"Was the 'child of the wind' crack or was it the gold doubloon he shoved at you the tip off?"

The woman ignored Scarlet's taunt, staring deeper into the crystal ball. She gasped, jerking away. "BEWARE!!!" she screeched, throwing wild gestures in the air.

Calix pressed his face against the crystal ball searching for the source of the panic. "What? What danger lies before us, seer?"

The woman grabbed both his shoulders, giving him a firm shake. "Many eyes are upon you! Desiring...

"Your death."

Calix plucked her bony fingers off, with care not to break them.

"That's it?" he asked, snatching the cotton candy from Scarlet.

"THAT'S IT?" The woman wailed.

Scarlet laughed and gave her a wink. "Sugar, it'd be more shocking for you to tell him someone *doesn't* want us dead. Come on, Calix, you haven't seen El Dorado yet."

As Scarlet led Calix toward the carousel, he leaned down to whisper in her ear. "I don't think that woman was a real mage."

Scarlet quirked a grin. "You should've caught that the moment she implied we're involved....*romantically.*"

"Is that what she meant by couple?"

Scarlet hopped onto El Dorado, the three tiered Carousel. A pig on the middle tier caught her eye—short legs curled beneath a fat pink body in anticipation. Calix reluctantly picked the pig's partner.

"Strange choice for a race. Though for you the height is

proper."

Scarlet stroked the pig between the ears. "You obviously haven't tried to catch a greased hog." Her eyes traveled past Calix on the tier above them. Leaning over the necks of their horses, two men were taking great interest in her conversation. Calix's voice drew her back.

"Is that another mortal custom?"

"Yeah, mostly down south where my Ma came from."

One of the men laughed. "You're from the south? Could've fooled me with Bojangles here, Shirley."

The organ roared to life, a starting shot to awaken the carousel's menagerie. The race was off to a sluggish start. Calix pulled up to his full height, barely reaching the chest of the horses on the upper tier. "I'm assuming that was an insult, secretary?"

The horses took off, charging past the bounding pigs. "Secretary?" The men yelled behind them, "The south really that backwards?" The horses bounded forward too fast. They leapt from their steeds, stumbling toward the middle tier.

Scarlet growled, "Hey cut that out, fellas. I don't wanna start anything."

Calix slid off his mount, heading toward the men. "No need to start it yourself, secretary. When I am through, Cunning Aryx will be indistinguishable from Sedes the Lyrical!" Calix charged toward their waiting fists. A sharp tug at his mind pulled him up on the upper tier. Scarlet clung to his arm as they shot past the attackers. Calix grumbled. "First time I've seen you *cower* from a fight, child of wind."

"Doing this for their sake, not yours." The men leapt

onto the upper tier, the speed knocking them off their feet. "See? Pitiful. Not worth the jail time."

Calix wrenched his arm away. "We'd be imprisoned for doing this realm a service?" A well timed kick landed both men back on the middle tier. He jumped down after them. Scarlet followed suit.

"Hey remember that time you said you wanted to learn how to blend in? This ain't how it's done." A couple of young ladies squealed, and clung desperately to their sheep, as Scarlet ran past. One of the men rolled away from another kick from Calix, landing hard on the slowest tier. He scratched at the man's face in the most dragonish way.

The man punched Calix directly in the face.

"Oh. That's how it works," he hissed.

The other jumped to his feet. Catching the idea of it, Calix pulled back his arm, nearly catching Scarlet in the face with his elbow. His fist found an eye, knocking the man over the head of a hog. He fell to the lower tier, head inches from where the spinning floors met.

Another tug on Calix's mind turned him to Scarlet.

"Happy now?" She latched onto his wrist, pulling him toward the exit. The hesitant curiosity of the crowd was melting into fear. Scarlet could almost hear the police sirens.

"Nice to see mortals enjoying a good fight as much as a dragon does. I like this realm." The men met them at the exit, the crowd giving both parties a wide berth. Scarlet pushed Calix through the open gate then turned to them. She snapped her fingers in front of their faces and their eyes glazed over. She fled, resuming her hold on the Dragon Lord.

"Temporary freeze, good as I can get without more effort. Far as they know we disappeared. The question is, where to? Preferably somewhere that won't land us in the hoosegow."

"Scarlet!" He called, eyes wide and grin wider. "What is this cave before us?"

She jolted at his sudden cry, following his gaze. "Uh. It's called a Tunnel of Love. It's for couples."

"There's a boat!"

"For couples."

"What's inside the mystery cavern?"

"*For couples.*"

"LET'S EXPLORE IT."

He dumped Scarlet into the boat, jumping in after her. Scarlet groaned, burying her face in her hands. The boat crawled forward by a creaky cable hidden under the water. Calix laughed, "What, secretary, afraid of the dark?"

"No, just what people think a guy and a gal do in the dark."

"What do they do?"

SPLASH!

Waves from the entrance slammed against their boat. Calix heard Scarlet scramble for a hold. She sighed. "Oh Lord, they found us."

"How? We hid in the cave."

Scarlet cast him a glare that was lost in the darkness. But Calix could hear it in her sharp tone and felt it searing into his mind. "Maybe they followed the crowd." Any further retort was cut short. The boat rocked as Calix's weight was hauled up and over the edge. Calix's fear bit into her mind. His consciousness began to slip away. In the darkness she couldn't reach his attacker. Not physically.

"Bad idea, boys," she hissed. The air crackled. "You forgot that Shirley knows how to dance too." She tore into their minds, unleashing images of nightmares only found in the realm of magic. Their muscles betrayed them, releasing Calix. He reached out for her. Scarlet pulled him back into the boat. It rocked violently. He leaned against the side, gasping for breath.

Scarlet gave him a sympathetic pat on the back. "Hard to fight what you can't see."

Calix chuckled. His golden eyes began to glow, Scarlet saw his pupils turn to reptilian slits. "Now that's a problem I can solve."

The end of the Tunnel of Love was a popular spot. A healthy crowd always gathered, hoping to catch a glimpse of young lovers. What, anywhere else, would be considered indecent was entertainment here. This time, the peeping toms got more than they bargained for. Young couples leapt from their boats, scrambling for the exit. Flames burst from the tunnel, licking at the churning waves. A single boat crawled into view. Calix and Scarlet stood at each end, crossing their own personal Delaware. Their attackers could only cling to the sides, trying in vain to dodge fists, feet, and the occasional flame.

Calix didn't realize how much he cherished his scales until now, as he lounged outside the entrance to his quarters. He stretched his long body to its limit, not wanting to waste any ray of the magic-blessed sun of his kingdom.

"Secretary!" He called, "Cancel all meetings, jailbreaks

are exhausting." He felt a buzz at the back of his mind, a small affirmation. Calix frowned, narrowing his eyes. "Too exhausted from whipping mortals to give me a proper answer?"

Another buzz, this one less gentle.

"You know I hate your mind games, empath. Come out where I can see you and speak to me like a proper secretary."

No buzzing this time, a small voice echoed within the cave. "Yes, oh great destroyer of love and its tunnel, you ask and I obey. Happy now?"

Calix picked at his teeth with a claw, "No, mage mutt, sinker of small boats. I wish to see your pale face when you speak to me."

There was a whisper of movement from the shadows and a mutter that Calix only caught a few words of. Something about a lack of pale. Scarlet stepped out into the sun, hissing like a basilisk drawn out of its cave. Calix's eyes widened.

"Are magi...supposed to be red?" he asked, studying her new skin tone.

Scarlet sighed and stepped back into the shadows. "No. It's called a sunburn. I forgot to put on sunscreen."

Calix threw his head back and laughed. "You mean to tell me that your kind is so weak that the sun herself can harm you?"

"Just the really pale ones." Scarlet corrected, scratching her itching neck.

Calix laughed harder, cinnamon smoke pouring from his nostrils. "And those men claimed that the pale skin was superior!"

Chapter 7

The spicy sweet cinnamon smoke mingled with the powerful scent of leather-bound books and crisp paper pages. Calix's low rumbling thrum provided harmony to the pop and crackle of a record player. His secret hoard felt so...warm. For the first time, Scarlet sensed Calix's mind at ease.

"Ah, Miss Scarlet, you have impeccable timing. I was just about to summon you." Calix glanced up from the book he held gingerly between his gold sheathed claws. A cryptic grin parted his scaly lips.

Scarlet quirked a brow. "Oh? Treasury need polishing? More yelling from that shield? Wanna go swing dancing at Coney Island?" She maneuvered around the stacks of books, catching a glimpse of the titles as she passed.

The Dynamics of an Asteroid
The Man of Bronze
The Federalist Papers

Calix shook his head. "No. Only some friendly discussion. I highly doubt anyone but you would be interested in my current hobby."

Scarlet plucked the book from his claws, it fit neatly in her hand. Her eyes traveled up the thin spine, *The Everlasting Man*. She chuckled. "No, I don't think your loyal subjects would understand your newfound appreciation for mortal culture. What, no classics of antiquity? I was sure *St. George and the Dragon* would be an instant hit."

Calix's thick scales shrugged off her barb. "No, Middle Ages are far beyond *your* age."

Scarlet squeaked. "My *age*? You don't even know my age."

Calix's cryptic smile grew. "It's written all over you. Your dress is new; it certainly doesn't match any of the illustrations. Too much color, for second. Old ones grey and grey until they like black and only black. " He rolled the words over his plated tongue, pondering each one. "Your words are eclectic, cobbled. Hoarded and delivered with a flippancy that only comes with careful consideration. Above all, your voice. One that could only have been forged in the fires of the Wild West, seared under the spotlight of the Follies, smoked in the speakeasies of the Roaring Twenties. In other words, young."

"Well, you've certainly done your homework, sir." Scarlet snatched up a comic from his scattered pile. As she flipped through the pages of *Journey Into Mystery*, her voice dipped into that sugar sweet drawl. "Sooooo....ya like my singin' voice?"

Calix rested his muzzle against her, squinting to study the panels. "Yes, it is quite lovely."

From outside the safety of his secret hoard came a keening sound, at first soft and low but it grew and grew until it shook the mountain more than his roar ever could. A flurry of emotion overwhelmed Scarlet's senses, the force of it tore deep into her heart. Calix kept silent, listening, but wrapped his tail around his secretary.

"What is that?" Scarlet asked.

"I think your kind would call it...wailing."

Aurum burst through the tunnels, cloaked in smoke and fire. Her eyes wild, crest of spines raised on end. From that turbulent sea of emotion Scarlet picked up rage. "While the Great—while our mother sunned herself atop Aida's Watch, a mage stole into our nests. He fought the mothers and crushed their eggs."

Calix rose to his feet, releasing Scarlet. He spoke slowly. "Were there no sentries posted?"

"There were, but all turned outward. None expected a threat from within." Aurum's gaze fell on Scarlet, who gasped and pulled back.

Calix growled. "You dare accuse my own secretary of this crime?"

"No, no," Scarlet interrupted, "she means…"

Scarlet dashed past shelves, knocking over the record player in her frantic haste. Out into the hoard, scattering treasure she had so carefully arranged. She staggered, reeling, grasping for those invisible threads she once followed.

She found it on the edge of his hoard: the cursed shield. A dent fractured the delicate lines, no longer glowing. Her eyes traced past piles of gold and gems, she saw the holes left by stumbling feet. A flash of rage sent shockwaves through the hoard, a furious burst of the empath's magic. Then, quickly, it pulled back and Scarlet, with a deep breath, went cool once more.

Aurum, who had watched with Calix, filled the silence. "No, she didn't crush our eggs. But she *is* responsible."

Scarlet turned to Calix, fighting back tears. "It was old. And fragile. I threw it. I hit you. I broke the enchantment."

Aurum's tail lashed. "He came here for *you. You* let him

live. *You* made our lord weak. *You,* who know our ways so much better, will be the end of them all." She turned to Calix, pleading, "Lord—brother—please. Come away from your books. Stop holing up with this mage. Save what's left of your own kind."

Calix stirred from his stupor. "It would have been better for that Knight to steal from my own hoard."

Scarlet stepped forward. "Please, my lord, my dear friend. I caused this. Let me fix it. Let me redeem myself."

Aurum spat. "You've done enough! Calix, stop letting this mage fight your battles."

"Calix, that Knight is going for Firetail. You don't know him. I do. My sister knows the Magi Council, she can talk to them. We can negotiate."

Aurum hissed. "*Dragons do not negotiate wars,* we end them."

The dragons could feel Scarlet's magic build. Calix saw how hard she fought to contain it. "It's not a war yet. Let me try and keep it that way."

Aurum flared. "Let you? You overstep your bounds, mage. Calix, we must strike first."

Scarlet's magic stirred, but she kept even, voice too low for them to hear. "No."

Calix kept quiet, but smoke poured from his clenched fangs.

Aurum snapped her jaw. "That mage made you too sentimental. Strike before that general comes, show your might."

"*No,*" this time a bit louder, firmer.

"Force them back."

"*No*," Scarlet's magic made the room quiver.

Calix snarled but still didn't speak.

"Make them fear."

"**NO!**"

Calix growled low in his throat, "Silence."

"Calix, please! I've heard this all before. This never ends well. Please, listen to me."

The growl grew louder. "I've listened enough."

Aurum cut between Scarlet and Calix. "They're just like any other pest, my lord. You let one in, and an infestation follows. They will not leave until they've all burned."

"Calix you burn those towns and you're no better than them. You're victims now, don't make more. They won't fear you, they'll hate you."

Calix roared, "**HATE ME?** *THEY'LL* **HATE** *ME*?" He rose up, wings flared wide. He lashed forward, covering himself in smoke and fire. Scarlet clutched at her head, reeling back. "**YOUR BLASTED PEACE LEFT US VULNERABLE, MY TRUST IN YOU COST MY KIN THEIR OWN CHILDREN. YES, HELLHOUND, THEY'LL HATE ME. BUT NOWHERE NEAR HOW MUCH I HATE THEM. FIVE MAGI BURN FOR EVERY ONE OF MY LOST HATCHLINGS. WOULD YOU LIKE ME TO START WITH YOU?**"

Scarlet turned and ran. A burst of flame hit the treasure beside her. Molten gold splattered up and burned into her leg. She stumbled but kept running, out the room and down the tunnels. Calix was not far behind. She felt the heat of his flame, but didn't turn to look. She heard his claws tearing gashes in the rock, and sensed how badly he wanted them in her.

The dragons on the shelf of Leviathan's Peak made room for her and the Dragon Lord. They watched, but didn't interfere. The wailing melted into a deep, earth shaking growl. A tail lashed out and caught Scarlet across the legs. She tumbled forward, and nearly off the edge of the plateau. On her back, Scarlet looked up into the face of the nesting mother whose mouth she once bound. Calix's roar brought back her senses. She forsook the dragon-filled shelves and began hopping from pillar to pillar. Bursts of Calix's fire slammed into each one as she left it. She took a chance and leapt off the pillars onto the Cracked Lands below and ended up slamming her shoulder into the dry earth.

She leapt to her feet and kept running, knowing all the while that dragons fly much faster than they run. More bursts of flame kept her close to the edge of Aikon's Flight, forcing her to slow or join the wyvern she once fought. Calix's rage was too strong for her magic; she didn't have the power to force his mind, or the desire to rip it to shreds. She felt him close in before she saw the shadow or felt the wind whipped up by wings. He snatched her up in his claws.

Calix dropped her deep in the Cracked Lands, far beyond the borders that allowed her to teleport home. "Go find the city of Leviathan and Aida, find some mercy *there.*"

In silence Scarlet watched him leave. A snap of her fingers brought her notepad. With a sigh she read the to-do list.

Free Knight from cursed treasure.
Check.

Chapter 8

Scarlet sighed as she consulted her schedule. A dragon could fly in hours what any land-locked race would take weeks to travel. After a quick calculation, she realized by the time she reached Leviathan's Peak, the war would have started. It was inescapable. She could only hope to minimize the damage.

She gave a sharp whistle. Nothing stirred. She pursed her lips and snapped her fingers. Still nothing. Under her breath she cursed the unreliability of "magical mounts" and began walking. It wasn't long before she heard the rhythmic *thud-thud* of hooves on sand and turned to find a horse trotting by her side. She arched a brow. "Had your laugh?"

The chestnut stallion flicked his ears.

"Gonna give me a ride now?"

He came to a stop and watched her, chewing on his bit. She put her hands on her hips and closed the gap, inspecting his saddle and reins. She opened the saddlebag and rifled through the supplies. "Gambled away any of my stuff?"

He swiveled his ears back toward her. She glanced up and narrowed her eyes at him. "Should've invested in a unicorn. They don't pawn off my clothes." The stallion snorted and stamped his hoof. She laughed.

"Alright, alright, Mischief. Enough joshin' around. Let's get to work."

Caravans carved routes through the Cracked Lands as they searched for secrets the harsh desert kept close to its heart. They knew where the waters hid, what caverns had not been claimed by the wyverns, where ruins of strongholds stood as testaments to kingdoms long forgotten. Scarlet, however, had no such luck. Sand and scrub for miles around, and jagged red rocks burst from the dry earth, providing what little shade was left this far.

Shade, but no water.

It was fine the first few days. She sucked on a pebble to keep her mouth from drying out. But that only worked for so long. She could feel her skin burning again, and swore to "the merciful not-dragon Lord above" that she would always carry sunscreen from then on out.

If she made it out.

She was starting to question that.

Slumped against Mischief's neck, she hummed in time with his slowing steps. Flickers of life stirred at the corner of her mind. A lizard scurried across the sand. A bird wheeled overhead. A jackalope taunted her from the twigs of a dead bush.

That grinning jerk knew where water was, but darned if he'd tell.

"I'd wipe that bucktooth smirk off your ugly mug," she croaked, "if I had half a mind to get my rifle out of my bag."

Mischief walked past the scrub.

"You think you're safe because you're a small target. But I'm a dead shot. Like Annie Oakley. But better."

Mischief gave a derisive snort.

"Okay. Close. I'm close. Never could shoot the card in

half."

Scarlet turned from glowering at the jackalope, bringing her attention back to him. She watched his ears swivel. "I'm a good hunter, you know. The best. Teddy said so. You were there when he said it, right? Teddy. Roosevelt. We hunted the White Stag, remember? Best game for the best hunters."

Her gaze wandered, she stared hard into the waves of heat dancing off the cracks in the earth.

"We caught him too. Not that anyone'd believe us. Farfetched, even for me."

Something stirred in the dust, it glimmered amidst the sun's harsh reflection. She squinted and thought she saw the light streaming between milky white horns.

"We let him go." Her voice had dropped to a whisper. "Just wouldn't be right, mounting his head on a wall."

There he was, secure in a glory that had not dimmed in the half-century since she caught him, or the millennia since Camelot. The Stag was massive, and when he rattled his antlers the sky shook with laughing thunder. His pelt was not merely some shade of white; it was something positive and essential, as necessary as starfire to the night sky. To see the Stag was to desire it, instinctually.

Jerking the reins, she guided Mischief toward it. He gnawed the bit, but followed her lead.

"He belongs out there. Alive. Running."

The dust was choking, she didn't even think to fish for her kerchief. If she turned away, she might lose sight of him.

She sighed. "Maybe I'm not that great a hunter."

She slumped in the saddle again, head against

Mischief's neck. The dust had settled, leaving nothing behind but more sand and scrub.

And the fresh tracks of a caravan's cart.

She reached their campout in the evening, when predators took advantage of the cool air and the blindness of its prey.

An old centaur met her with a warm greeting and a brandished lance. "Hail, stranger. You speak to Abaco. What brings a wanderer this far out in the wastes?"

She glanced over his gray flank and old, but well-kept armor. He had all the markings of an experienced soldier. "A very angry dragon." She flashed a smile, holding up both hands to show the only thing she held was the reins. Abaco didn't lower his weapon; empty hands made a mage no less dangerous to deal with.

"You didn't bring it with you, I hope." He glanced toward the skies and stamped a hoof.

"Ah, no. He had other things to take care of. So do I. What's the quickest way to civilization?" She leaned forward, resting an elbow on her saddle horn as she watched him.

"The quickest way is not the safest. Leads through death worm territory. Even wyverns refuse to fly over it. The better route is through the canyon. It'll add a few days, but its walls will protect you from the worst threats."

Scarlet sighed. "That's always the way, isn't it? Safe or quick. Never both. Alright, point me to the death worms. And if you have any supplies you'd be willing to part with, I'm happy to pay you for it."

She looked past the centaur. By this point, many of the group had stepped out of their camp, some with dinner plates still in their hands. It was a small group, mostly centaurs with a few magi. All armed with the traditional weapons of the soldiers of the mage army. Polearms and lances, the favored method of keeping the opponent at bay, with swords and shields for when that failed. Most had an alert gaze, constantly scanning the horizon. The way one did when they were used to being hunted. They watched Scarlet with interest, some laughed at her answer. The centaur cocked his head, studying her. "You risk much."

"I have a habit of that. Good thing I enjoy gambling." She quirked a wry grin.

He shook his head. "Your life and your gold mean nothing to me. Water and food are too precious to waste on someone digging their own grave."

Twisting around, she dug through her saddlebags once more. "Perhaps you can profit off my wild, reckless ways. When you deserted whatever post you kept, I'm sure you left some things behind." The soldiers shifted, the centaurs stamped. She didn't glance up, pulling all manner of glowing crystals out of her bag. "My father is an enchanter, I always keep a few essentials of his trade in my bag. I don't know what sort of magic y'all wield, but I don't know a single mage who couldn't find some use out of a few enchanting crystals. Let's see. You live in a desert, would some frost ones help cool things down? Your shields' protective runes look a bit worn, I have a few barrier crystals that should recharge them. I only have one illusion breaker, but it should last quite a while as long as you don't use it all over creation."

She glanced up to find them staring at her in wonder.

Abaco drew near. "Luxuries of the capitol. The sort of

things only given to the most valuable knights and captains. Not something I ever expected to see with my own eyes."

Mischief pulled his ears back stepping away from the lance. Scarlet kept her eyes on him, scanning the surface of his mind, searching for any indication of treachery. "You're an old soldier. Must have deserted during the last war. What turned your stomach first? Burning the sylph's forests? Rounding up the minotaurs? Or did you stay long enough to take elvish lands?"

Abaco paused, his face growing grim. "I am not Firetail. I took no orders from him. I fought honorably, to protect the land I was born in. I took nothing that didn't belong to me."

Scarlet relaxed, offering him another smile. "Well then, I trust you to make me a fair trade."

The crystals had gained her a safe night in their camp and a week's worth of water and food—more than she hoped she would need. They offered her a few sturdy weapons, all of which she turned down with the claim that she had everything she needed to handle whatever threats came her way. The soldiers laughed, but made no more offers. In the morning they pointed her in the right direction, the straightest route through death worm territory to the mountain range that lead to Leviathan's Peak.

The worms were most active in the morning, Abaco warned.

"Ah, such is the fate of the early bird."

Scarlet's joke was lost on the centaur.

She wasted no time, heading off after breakfast. It was quick riding, since the terrain was mostly comprised of flat plains of nothing—nothing but scrubs and the occasional sandy hill. She sensed the occasional spark of life, some wandering wild thing that was sure to keep its distance. Mischief's ears swiveled constantly. He didn't stop to nibble at every bush, never even bothered to rip the reins out of her hands. All of which was very odd.

"You know we're perfectly safe, right?"

He snorted.

"No. I mean it. I am more than qualified to handle death worms. It's in my resume. Under my expedition experience. I dealt with plenty of the Mongolian variety back when I used to pal around with Roy Chapman Andrews. Not that he ever believed me. They never showed up when he was in the vicinity."

He continued to trot along.

"That's supposed to be impressive, you know. Roy. Chapman. Andrews. Former director of the American Museum of Natural History. Famous explorer. Author of important books. Would've written me a recommendation letter if he hadn't already, you know, passed on."

Another snort. Long and drawn out.

Scarlet frowned. "You, my friend, lack the culture to appreciate such acquaintances. Or maybe you're just jealous, since the most famous fella you ever knew was *Seabiscuit*. And he liked me better."

Mischief's head snapped up, his pace quickened. She laughed and gave his neck a fond pat. Twisting around in the saddle, she flipped open the saddlebag and pulled out a Winchester 1873 Lever-Action Rifle from its seemingly bottomless depths—and started chambering rounds.

"Good Lord bless enchanted storage. Not wise to keep a

gun in plain sight around this realm. Magic folk don't know what to do with mortal contraptions. But I'll tell you what, sure beats a lance. Less taxing, more immediate than magic."

She saw the shifting sand out of the corner of her eye. Worms had barely any mind to speak of, nothing there for her to sense, certainly nothing to influence. She watched the ripples in the sand, like the wake of an invisible boat. "Three feet long." She mumbled to herself. "Not seven. That's good."

She dropped the reins, readied her rifle. "You know where you're going."

Mischief kept on, but she heard his breathing quicken. His ears twitched. The ripples kept parallel, matching his pace. She measured the distance between them. "Eight feet." She hummed. "Keep on trottin', don't speed up. You'll get it all excited. Don't think it knows we're onto it."

Despite the bounce of the saddle, she kept the barrel trained on the crest of the wave.

"Seven feet now. Steady."

She worked the lever and settled her finger on the trigger.

"Six. *Run*."

Mischief took off. Years of experience were the only thing keeping her in the saddle. A sharp snap. Electric sparks lanced across the sand, bounding in short angry arcs. Mischief brayed.

"Oh come on now, if I had told you they were slimy tesla-coils, you would've been a bundle of nerves." The wave of sand rose higher, veering behind them. The rifle followed. Mischief snorted. Her lip twitched upward. "Well, yeah. Now you *should* be. Puts a spring in your step."

It burst from the sand, a blur of blood red against the cloudless sky.

"Left!" She barked, pulling the trigger.

CRACK!

Mischief jerked to the left. Acid gushed past his flank, tearing into the earth where he had almost been. The bullet ripped through slimy flesh; the remains of the worm smashed against the ground. Scarlet laughed and turned back around, fishing for the reins she dropped. "Nasty bits of leaping haggis. Nothin' to it."

Mischief pulled his head back, his screech pulled her attention back up. She didn't have time to count the rippling waves before them. Mischief veered to the right in a mad gallop.

"Packs? They hunt in packs?" She yelped, "That's not what they did in the Gobi."

He brayed.

"Yes. I'm aware we're not in Mongolia. Thank you, Columbus."

She worked the lever on her rifle and brought it to bear on the closest worm. Two launched into the air, spewing acid. Her bullets tore them both apart.

"Just like shootin' skeet." Her rifle swept to the right and blasted another from the sky.

"Hey, mountains. Go. We're nearly there. They can't burrow in rock."

Her instructions weren't needed, he was already running in that direction.

"Just thought you'd like to know. We've got a few comin' up behind too. If you have a higher gear, might wanna shift into it."

Three burst from the sand to their left, each bullet ripped them apart. The sand was now churning, electric arcs dancing across the countless waves, acid and blood bubbling. She had loaded fourteen rounds, fired seven. Seven rounds left.

One worm leapt from behind.

Six now.

Not nearly enough.

Three from the right.

Three left.

"You better be glad I'm a good shot." She growled at Mischief, venturing a glance toward the mountain range. They were closing in, close enough that the sand before them was calm. She patted her rifle, "C'mon, honey, you're the '*Gun That Won the West.*' Let's not shame Winchester's great name."

Two from the left and three behind.

"Left!" She barked, already training her rifle behind. Mischief veered on command, underneath the two worm's arc. She blasted the three. The barrel was still smoking as she chambered the next round.

Another pack leapt before she was finished, three to the right. She snapped the rifle up, worked the lever, and fired. The first two hit the ground, but the third managed to spew its acid before she blew it apart. Mischief dodged the worst, but flecks of the spray burned into her arm and his flank.

"Not tryin' to be pushy, but it would be great if we could make our escape before I have to reload again."

Chapter 9

By the time they reached the shadow of the mountains, the swarm had thinned and the worms decided she wasn't worth the effort. Mischief kept on until he felt safe amongst the rocks. A quick stop for lunch, and a light salve for their burns, and they took off again. The next few days were not nearly as exciting, something both considered rather positive.

Leviathan's Peak loomed high in the corner of her eye, far to her left, alight with fire, cloaked in swirling smoke, a sign to the realm of the dragons ire. More days passed before they reached the magi borders. Towns were already ash. Scarlet's marching tunes and idle chatter faded away. The rest of the trip was spent in silence.

Deeper into the mage territory the plains became greener, and the world began to breathe again. But it remained quiet. Stifling. Eyes were on her; she felt them burning. She fished in her pack for a cloak, which she threw over her shoulders.

An outpost on the horizon proved the source of her foreboding. Unfinished—hastily built from the forest behind. On the watchtower she spotted the glint of metal. Within, she heard the screech of gryphons and the stirring of soldiers.

That was all she needed to know. The gryphonriders, pride of the mage army, had come to protect their lands. If anyone could take down a dragon, it would be them. She gave the outpost a wide berth, turning right and heading toward the source of life she pegged as the closest surviving town. Refugees camped by the borders.

They ignored her, continuing conversations she caught snippets of.

"—low race filth bringing all their diseases with them."

"—without a warning. Beasts burned the whole town in minutes."

"—noble knight went in to save that girl. Turns out she'd been working for those lizards all along. She's more of a beast than they are."

Scarlet spurred Mischief on, pulling her cloak tighter. Their pain seared her mind.

"—she betrayed us."

She spotted a minotaur at the fringe of the camps, his thick hide blackened. He nursed a warm cup in his hands and watched as she cut through the chaos.

"I am clean, little one," he rumbled as she drew near. "No sickness. No lice."

"I know." Scarlet pulled Mischief to a stop. She smiled.

He tapped a horn, their version of tipping a cap. "Do you need assistance?"

"Just information. Where's the tavern?"

He pointed it out for her and wished her well. Before she left, she dug out some gold from her pack and leaned in, setting the coins in his large hands. "I'd find a safer town than this. Those magi...they're angry, and hurt, and will take it out on something. You're a mighty big target."

He nodded. "You're not all bad, little one."

She shrugged. "No race is."

When she left, the minotaur glanced down at the gold coins, nicked by claw marks. He recognized a dragon's treasure when he saw it. Glancing out to the refugees, then back to the gold. Without a word, he slipped the coins into his pocket and made off for greener pastures.

"Don't stray too far, don't gamble, and don't cause a stir. I'll be back soon."

Scarlet patted Mischief's muzzle and left him outside the tavern. Her entrance caused nothing but a few passing glances. She was just another refugee. She took a seat near the bard who was currently being drowned out by the din of raucous conversation. He strummed halfheartedly on his lyre, mumbling the lyrical praises of Sir Ascamore, Father of the Gryphonriders, slayer of monsters. Scarlet ordered some Minotaur Mead from a passing satyr waiter and sat back to listen to his song.

Sensing a new audience, the bard put on his winningest smile and drew near. "Hail, fair maid, from what tragedy do you seek refuge in this merry hall? By the look of your fine features, you must have many a tale worth telling. Or perhaps singing."

Scarlet crinkled her nose. "Boy, you sure lay it on thick." She took a sip of her mead. "Oh I doubt I'm half as interesting as all the grand tales you've rustled up. Surely a bard as talented as you has some stories of grand glories of the front line."

The bard grinned wider. "Certainly, m'lady, Malory is at your service." At a strum of his lyre, Scarlet sucked in a breath and braced herself for a song.

To her great relief, none came. Instead…

"So by fortune this damosel in dire dragon clutches heard tell that Sir Olwydd did much for damosels' sake; so she sent to him a pensel, and prayed him to fight with Volos the Terribly-Scaled for her love, and he should have her and her lands of her father's that should fall to her. Then the damosel sent unto Volos the Terribly-Scaled, and she gave him warning that she had sent Sir Olwydd her pensel, and if it might overcome Sir Olwydd she would wed him. When Volos the Terribly-Scaled wist of her deeds then was he wood wroth and angry, and passing faint, and flew with smoke and bristle unto Monarchisa where the haut prince Sir Olwydd was, and there he found Sir Olwydd ready, he which had the pensel. So there they would wage battle either with other. *Well*, said the haut prince Sir Olwydd, *this day must noble knights joust flaming wurms, but the sun wanes; let us yet at-after dinner see how ye can speed.* So they ate, Sir Olwydd to venison and Volos the Terribly-Scaled to a sheep he thieved from the nearest farm; but Sir Olwydd was a passing chivalrous knight and put paid to farmer for the flame and damage."

As her eyes began to glaze, and she ordered a stiffer drink, Malory found himself interrupted by a little old man who took a seat beside her. He raised his hat, then cast a significant glance at the bard, waiting until he shrunk back to resume his earlier song.

"Ah, Miss Chase, how good to see you traipsing about in the middle of all this mess."

She grinned. "Well, hello there, Dominie. What brings you to this backwater town?"

"Oh, you know me, I adore travel," he answered absently as he dug through his bottomless coat pockets, pulling out all manner of trinkets: scattered bits left-over from children's games; jacks and cards; coins in a dozen sizes, denominations, and origins; a signet ring surmounted by a pale blue crystal; any number of stolen spoons; a cork-sealed vial of water which shone like the sun; a necklace made of beads some mad jeweler had fashioned to look like commas escaping off their page; a scattered handful of barleycorns and beans; and a regrettable amount of pocket lint. "My plans, however, were interrupted by a bit of *drragonfire.*" He rolled the Rs for emphasis. "Nasty business."

Dominie pulled out a crinkled piece of parchment. The bard sidled closer to steal a glance over his shoulder only to be met with a withering glare.

"Yes," Scarlet answered, drawing the word out with a sigh. "Very nasty."

Dominie rifled through the pile of trinkets on the table, pulling out a set of glasses to inspect the parchment closer. "That mage who betrayed her own to serve those scaly brutes must regret her decision."

Scarlet shifted in her seat.

He didn't glance up.

"I don't know. I like to give everyone the benefit of a doubt. *Maaaaaybe* she was just trying to…" She waved a hand through the air. "Fix things."

Dominie eyed her over his glasses. "If so, she did a rather bad job of it."

Scarlet opened her mouth. Closed it. Tried again, and ended up downing the rest of her mead. "I didn't say she succeeded. Just that she might have tried."

"And what good does that do, hm? You're an empath, my dear, I know for you it's the thought that counts, but most in this realm prefer a bit of action."

Scarlet quirked a brow. "I'm not exactly a stranger to the concept."

"Yes. How foolish of me, to suppose such a gambler wouldn't know how to put her money where her cheque can't cash." He took off his glasses, tapping them to his lips. For a moment he pondered, then…

"How's your chess game, Miss Chase?"

Scarlet quirked a smile and leaned in. "I don't play chess, Dominie. You know that."

"And what sort of game do you play?" He asked, but the twinkle in his eye suggested he already knew. He slid the paper to her, and she gave it a passing glance.

An order intercepted from General Friesian himself, and from the looks of the plans, she had a hunch where she could find him.

"Like you said, I'm a gambler. I play poker."

Chapter 10

The gryphonriders vaulted over fallen knights. Bursts of flame melted shields. Scales shunted lances. Serrated beaks and feline claws ripped through wings. The elements bent to the will of their magi masters, and their fury turned on the dragons. The sky was painted by glittering scales and armor, colored flames and spells. The sun and moon both hung in the sky, one on each end of the battlefield. Gold and silver intertwined, gracing each combatant with a halo of light.

On the field below wounded magi struggled with grounded dragons. A whip of wind tore through wings. The Knight forced back dragons with the might of his magic. A lashing tail caught him across the face, slashing off his helmet as he downed one more of the mighty beasts. He leapt down from the smoking carcass to retrieve the helm, but something caught his eye.

A figure melted from the swirling smoke. The form of a figure warped by a cloak, riding a stallion that seemed to be made from golden sand. The steed glided toward the Knight, hooves never touching the seared grass. A spirit of the Cracked Lands, come to avenge the eggs shattered on its land. The Knight cried out, but no one heard. The spirit pressed forward, never flinching at the battle that raged around it.

No one saw the spirit in their midst.

No one but the Knight.

The world around him faded, a veil of smoke and muted

color bending around the spirit. It drew closer. The roar of battle dimmed, all except the spirit's song. The words burned his ears, their weight bound his legs. It sung of the days of Leviathan and Aida, forged from starfire. Mighty father of dragons who churned the mighty sea. Cunning rainbow serpent who set the clouds in motion. The spirit towered over him, and slipped off the back of its horse.

The spirit punched him in the face.

He fell back, getting a glimpse under the hood of a pale face. Fire crackling in eyes green like moss. Scarlet took a deep breath before she spoke.

"I'd like a word."

The Knight led Scarlet through his camp. The few magi not at the battle shrank from the strange spirit. Now, by her choice, she could be seen. Though her voice was soft, her song filled the camp. Neither she, nor her stallion, turned their gaze from the Knight. He could feel her eyes pierce his armor as they followed him to the war-tent. A servant stood watch. He stepped forward at the Knight's approach.

"Who comes?"

She pulled her steed in front of the Knight. "The Dragon Lord's Secretary."

"You speak with his authority?"

"I speak with authority."

The servant stared. She dismounted as he went inside. The servant returned, gesturing for them both to follow. Scarlet lowered her hood and swept through the entrance with as much regality as she could manage. Her eyes trailed upward. Black fur coated with a fine mist of rust. Dark-skinned chest encased in armor, the finest dwarven forged.

A shoulder-scabbard was modified to hold an enchanted brand whose head was always burning, the smell of hot metal always lingering. Equine eyes filled with predatory cunning, more than Scarlet had ever seen in a centaur's face. The Knight took up post beside him.

Firetail patted his sheathed brand. "You're unarmed, mage. Do you trust your own powers to protect you?"

She glanced between the two. "I have no intention of fighting. I'm in your camp. You'd win by numbers alone. Even Merlin couldn't have faced a whole army. Or else Camelot would still be around, I think."

The Knight relaxed some, but Friesian remained as alert as ever.

"Then what exactly do you think you're here for?"

She snapped her fingers and summoned a pair of glasses, a notepad, and a pen. Setting the glasses low on her nose, she jotted something down. "I'm here to negotiate the terms of your surrender. One mage might not be impressive, but an army of dragons is. I doubt you want to keep this up for much longer. Now tell me what you'd like and I'll send it up to my superiors. We'll talk this out like rational beings."

The Knight scoffed. "Those beasts aren't rational."

Scarlet took a seat. She rapped her nails against the wooden arm of the chair. "You know, I used to be afraid of knights. Silver men haunted my dreams."

Friesian flicked his short-cropped tail. "You've come far to speak in riddles. Is wasting my time a new strategy of the Dragon Lord's?"

She glanced around the room, eyes resting on the Knight.

He shifted, glancing to his superior. The general stamped his hoof. He turned to the secretary. The warm light robbed her of that otherworldliness. Now she was only a freckled face in a cape just a bit too large. Her nails continued to beat out a rhythm against the wooden chair. Strange, perhaps, but not threatening. That rhythm wormed its way into his head. He cleared his throat and rubbed his bloody nose.

"You're not scared of them now," the Knight said.

Miss Chase quirked a smile. "No. I became one." She paused, then spoke slowly, words matching the rhythm of her nails. "Not so impressive under that armor. Just a mage. Usually with something to prove. Same with generals."

Friesian flicked his tail, a blur of black rimmed with rust. "I have nothing to prove. I end wars."

"You *lose* wars to be more precise." Her eyes never left the Knight. He could feel her pale green eyes boring through, piercing his skull. "That old war started to protect our borders, General Friesian, but once that claim was staked, you turned to conquering. You failed. Your glory days are gone. You're old hat now, Firetail. No more burning towns for you. Why don't we try negotiating instead?"

Friesian reared up, slamming his front hooves on the ground. "I still live, lizard lover. More than can be said for The Errant. Where did he go, that pride of the low races? The turner of tides? The war ends, and he leaves them to pick up the shambles."

Scarlet's eyes snapped up to the general towering over her. Her face grew hard. "The Errant? General, you and I both know better than to believe in legends. We're all that's left of that mess, and starting another war isn't gonna clean it up."

Friesian pawed at the ground. Iron-shod hooves tore gashes in the earth. He called forth his servant from a quiet corner. "For someone so concerned about my razing of villages, you don't seem affected by the victims of a dragon raid." General Friesian threw back the hood of his servant. Thick bandages stuck to the charred flesh that remained on a face burnt beyond recognition.

Friesian laughed. "Go on, mage, explain to him why you sold yourself to the beasts who roast your kind alive." He shoved the servant at her.

She stared into his face, wide-eyed. "Oh. Royal flush."

The servant shrunk back, bowing his head.

Gathering her composure once more, Scarlet turned to the Knight. "*You* crushed eggs." She gestured out of the tent. "Those dragons burned towns that stole their land. *They* pulled back, *they* made this a cold war, *you* warmed it back up." Her soft voice pounded in their heads.

Friesian paced, drawing closer to her. "You are a traitor to your own race!"

The Knight hesitated. "…I did what I had to. That was an army's worth of eggs. They were only dragons. Inhospitable, soulless creatures. That mother told you to burn, Miss Chase, and her children were destined to make sure of it."

Scarlet stood, stepping back from Friesian. "You don't fight dragonfire with your own fire. I understand, you had to defend your towns. But in this war, no one wins. Everyone will burn." She looked to the Knight. "This all started because you wanted to be a hero. You wanted to save me, remember? You still have that chance. You can still stop this. No one else has to die today. Talk to the Dragon Lord. He's angry, he's hurt, but he will listen to reason. He will negotiate."

The Knight looked to Friesian. "Sir. If that's possible—"

"Your race has always been spineless. You're swayed by such simple words. I'll make sure you speak no more, secretary. You'll poison no more minds."

Scarlet gritted her teeth. "I can't take your whole camp, General. But if I'm going to die here, I'll make sure you're coming along."

She hadn't finished speaking before he reared up, lashing out.

"Guards!"

He rushed forward, and in the same sweeping movement he pulled his brand from the scabbard on his back and thrust down at her. She crashed over backwards. The brand's blistered-cherry head smoldered in her robes, throwing up woolen sparks. She was an inch too low.

He reared back, coiling for another thrust.

An empath might have early warning—but warnings don't count in cramped quarters. She rolled away from the brand, crashing into the general's table. His brand seared a patch of her robe black. No room left to dodge. Scrabbling hooves brought him closer, blocking her into the tight space.

Friesian stamped for stable ground and rolled his arm back, the mark of the brand aimed perfectly for her stomach. He drove the brand down.

But his arm caught midway, and he turned his head, snarling.

The servant held his arm. Friesian batted him away with the same arm, a wicked backhand across the face. The servant, however, did not fall away. He held onto the arm—gripping it, twisting it away from Friesian even as Friesian raised his left fist and smashed it into the servant's face.

Scarlet turned to the Knight, who stood still, apparently in shock. An empath works like a needle through fabric. One stitch means nothing. Two stitches mean nothing. But give her enough time to sew deep enough, and far enough, and she can turn it any which way. She tugged on the thread she'd been working into his mind since the first time they met that night—and yanked.

"Sorry, sugar. But I can use this better than you."

She splayed her fingers out, and jerked them back. The Knight snapped to action, muscle memory filling in the gaps in her command. He lashed his arms out, wind stirring into strands across his palm.

Scarlet jerked her fingers closed. The winds fled the Knight's fists.

Friesian never had the chance for a second punch.

The Knight walked forward, inexorable. Whips sung out, wind finding a degree of form as they snapped like December's bitterest winds. These whips stung Friesian's legs. Then the winds rushed faster, slashing at his legs with razor cuts.

Nothing is more fragile than a centaur's legs. Suddenly, none of his legs could hold him upright, and he crumpled at the servant's feet.

"Guards," he hissed.

The camp flared into uproar. Shadows pantomimed

across the tent walls. Here a dozen men with swords, there a dozen men with staffs, and now men running by with ethereal weapons that refused to cast shadows. They seemed to be gathering, preparing a quick push into the tent.

"Never would have pegged you for servitude...or subterfuge." Scarlet met the servant's eyes.

"I am capable of many things you would not...peg me...for. Such things are beneath me, but at times one must make sacrifices. This sacrifice may end up more permanent than I hoped."

"Did you read anything about the Alamo in those books of yours? Looks like we got one of those."

"Yes, I did, though I believe I should go out in a bigger blaze of glory. There's no need to constrain myself to this petty form now."

Voluminous smoke poured out from Leviathan's Fire, covering his body. The smoke washed away, and there was no trace of the man. Instead the Great and Glorious Dragon Lord Calix reared upright, ripping the tent out from its pegs and blasting it up into the weightless air with a flex of his wings. Never the one to pass up a dramatic reveal, he half turned his head to the breezing fabric and set it alight with a touch of dragonfire.

The knights stood stunned as cinders consumed the sky.

Calix would have breathed a wide swath of fire, cremating some mages and burning others as he set upon them with his claws. The mages would have crowded over their dead, swords and spears and magic at hand, hacking at him. Scarlet would have fended them off, taking up fallen weapons and tearing into minds.

But the Knight stepped over Friesian. "Stop. I have negotiated peace." He looked up at the swirling bits of tent. "That is...a dragon sign of agreement."

The knights paused where they were, weapons still raised. They spoke quietly among themselves, then louder, arguing.

"You know, I don't think I ever asked your name." Scarlet said, quietly.

"Brastius."

Flame reared up in the distance, burning against the night. It roared in at a phenomenal speed that shouldn't belong to something so massive. As it neared, there was no mistaking it, a massive, wingless dragon running across the plain.

The sky was black. Then fire exploded from every point of the night, the light of that fire revealing an armada of dragons.

They were not listlessly arranged, like the beasts they were credited to be. Aurum's Raiders attended to the four corners of camp, hanging back about a quarter mile. The Raiders were ranged perfectly side-by-side. If they let loose their dragonfire as one, there would not be a hairsbreadth spared between their patterns. They were absolutely silent.

Their wings beat twice—the momentary pause that clings to every predator of the sky.

As one they breathed flame and turned their blazes to the ground.

As one they began to fly forward, consuming the plain below them.

As one, they picked up speed.

Everything, save Calix, would burn.

As Aurum raced on the two dragons above her stilled their fire and she ran between two searing orange-white walls.

Calix shot dragonfire into the air. "**AURUM! HOLD! I HAVE NEGOTIATED PEACE. WITH SOME AID FROM MY SECRETARY—AND NONE FROM THAT STUPID KNIGHT.**"

Epilogue

"All in all, Secretary, I think it turned out well for everyone involved."

Sunlight, carried by the salty sea breeze, warmed the scales of the Dragon Lord. Scarlet hid in the shadow he made, smothering her arms with sunscreen.

"You mean, the beach was a good trade for all those towns you're letting magi rebuild?"

Calix snorted, drawing circles in the sand with his tail. "What use would we have with towns if we can't burn them? But *this* with all the sea to swim, fish to eat, sea serpents to wrestle. I think the magi got the short end of the deal, really."

Scarlet lowered her sunglasses, peering at Calix over the rims. "Honestly, I'm surprised you took the deal at all. I thought dragons didn't do diplomacy."

Calix stood and stretched, shaking off sand. Scarlet yelped as it fell onto her still sticky skin. "Well, walking around in their skin for a bit gave me a new perspective. I felt the heat of dragonfire. Even though it was only superficial, enough to convince Friesian I was a victim. For the first time I felt the pain I inflicted, and I understood their desire for revenge. Also, you told me you spoke with the Dragon Lord's authority. Who was I to argue?"

Scarlet jumped up. "Oh, uh, that was before I saw it was you. And technically, I only said I speak with authority. I never said it was yours. Just trying to look impressive, you know."

Calix lowered his head, studying her with one golden eye. "It looks good on you."

Scarlet hesitated. "What does?"

"Authority."

Leviathan and Aida

*Being the traditional draconic creation myth as recorded
in the Dragon Lord's library*

Back when the world was new and the stars blanketed the
night with their brilliance, the Great Smith looked down
upon the world he had forged and was saddened at the
coldness of the earth. The Smith looked to the stars with
their brilliant, beautiful flame and wished that their warmth
could reach the earth. He summoned the star we call Sun
forward to blanket the earth with her heat. The Sun burned
brightly with excitement, so honored was she to be chosen
by the Smith that forged her. At first the earth flourished
under such warmth, but soon the earth's tender skin was
burnt by Sun's intense flames. The ground cracked and
blistered, creating what we call mountains and crags.

The Sun in her distress pulled away from the earth,
leaving it once again in darkness. The Smith poured water
on the earth, soothing its burnt skin and filling many of the
cracks in the surface. He convinced the Sun to come back
and created a helpmate for her. From the void he crafted the
Moon and she cast a softer light. With its burnt ground
healed, the Smith brought forth plants and animals. The
Sun and Moon danced happily around the earth, surveying
with wonder all that the Smith forged.

But still, the Smith returned his attention to the
brilliance of the stars that shone so far from earth's reach. If
only such light could dance freely upon the ground without
fear of scorching all he made. Then the Smith reached out
to the starfire and forged from it the first dragon, whom he

called Leviathan. Leviathan's brilliance outshone even that of the Sun. He knew this, and his fire burned brightly because of it. To cool Leviathan's proud flame, the Smith placed him in the oceans to live for a time. He spoke to Leviathan, saying, "I have placed the world under your dominion, go and discover all that I have given you." Leviathan was overjoyed with his new home in the sea: challenging the dolphins to races, comparing teeth with the sharks. It was Leviathan, with a flick of his mighty tail, who set the seas to churning. With playful twists he formed the whirlpools.

While Leviathan played, the Smith stretched out his hand once more to the stars. This time he forged a dragon of cooler flame and named her Aida. She was dazzling to behold, scales shimmering like a rainbow. The Smith set her in the sky so that all could enjoy her beauty. He spoke to Aida, saying, "I have placed the world under your dominion, go and discover all that I have given you." The Smith then created the clouds that would serve as her bed. The Sun and Moon were upset that the clouds obstructed their view of the earth. Aida understood their concerns and with her powerful breath separated the clouds and set them in motion. So Aida invented the wind which now moves her beloved clouds. The Sun and Moon praised her cleverness and thanked her for her kindness.

Aida danced through the sky with her friends Sun and Moon and taught the birds to sing. In thanks the birds brought her news from the land below, which she watched from afar. The birds spread news of Aida's cleverness and kind heart to all the creatures of the land, and soon they brought their troubles to her. One day the birds brought her news from the trees of the earth. They had heard tales of water from the creatures who roamed the land. They wished to see this water for themselves and feel its cool touch, but the Smith had rooted them to the ground so that they would not wander. The trees asked if there was any way for Aida to bring water to them.

Aida pondered this a while, asking advice from Sun and Moon. They showed her the way to the place where water met the sky. Never having traveled to such a place made her nervous. She feared that if she fell from the sky into the water, she may never be able to find her way back. So she brought her favorite cloud with her for support. When her cloud touched the water it soaked the water up like a sponge. Aida squealed in surprise at the sudden wetness and heaviness of her cloud. Quickly she drew back, squeezing the water out of the cloud with her long tail. This inspired Aida, who gathered her clouds to her and dipped them into the sea.

When they had been filled with as much water as they could manage, Aida guided them over the land and wrung them out. So the trees learned of water and Aida invented rain. Aida adored the rain and made a game of herding her clouds and spraying water upon the land below. The fish in the ocean living near where the water met the sky were enraptured by Aida's beauty and leapt from the sea to get better glimpses of her. Some fish were as comfortable in the air as in the water that they themselves seemed to fly. News from these fish soon made their way to the great Leviathan who had been challenged by the stingrays to find the bottom of the ocean.

Leviathan was drawn to the place where water meets

sky, where he waited with the flying fish to catch a glimpse of the fabled beauty. He saw Aida as she brought her clouds to the water and was just as captured by her brilliance as the fish had been. As she drew near the water, Leviathan burst through in a powerful leap. He tried to land on the clouds, but he was too heavy and they burst under his weight. Aida laughed at the sight of Leviathan's folly, pulling her clouds up out of his reach.

"So you are the one whose flame burned so bright he was placed in the sea to cool," Aida said. "Sun and Moon told me of you once."

Leviathan was puzzled at this. "You speak to sister Sun and Moon? They never talked to me."

Aida laughed again. "You are too far away. Too far beneath the sea. I live closer, with only the air between us. Perhaps if you came to visit they would be more talkative."

"All I've known is the sea," Leviathan answered. "And as you can see, I am much too heavy to climb into the sky."

Aida pondered this a moment. "I know of a place called the land, which lies between sky and sea. I have never been there myself, but I watch it from my clouds. Perhaps if you traveled there you could find an answer to your problem. I am going there now if you would like me to show you the way."

Leviathan agreed to this and followed Aida to the land. Leviathan looked to the land and grew nervous. If he left the sea, would he ever be able to return? He looked up at the beautiful Aida and remembered all the stories of her warmth and wit. He decided if the land would bring him closer to her it would be worth the risk.

"How does one live on the land?" Leviathan asked.

"That I do not know. The birds send me messages from the land, but I have never set foot there," Aida answered. "Perhaps they could help you."

Aida called for the birds, who sent word to all the creatures of the land. They came to meet Leviathan and help. The horses taught him to walk and run with the legs he had once used to swim, the cats taught him how to walk softly so that he would not damage the tender earth.

All the while Aida watched with interest, but Leviathan could not persuade her to visit the land. All she knew was the sky. If she came down she might not have the strength to climb back up again. So Leviathan travelled across the earth, searching for a place where he might climb up to the sky. That was when he found the mountains which climbed higher than any tree he had seen. He sent the birds to Aida, who brought her to where the mountains rose from the land to pierce the sky. With such a bridge between sky and land Aida happily came down to Leviathan. The birds, happy that Aida could now visit their homes, taught Aida how to climb into the air with her wings.

Though this meant that Aida could meet the land wherever she wished, she still loved the mountains where Leviathan first called her down from the sky. From there the Sun and Moon would come and speak with her and Leviathan, animals from land could travel to meet them, even Leviathan's friends the fish would travel up the streams to pay a visit. So Leviathan carved a home within the heart of the mountain and asked her to stay with him for the rest of her days. The clever and kind Aida had grown to love the proud and playful Leviathan, and so she agreed. The flames they kindled in their hearts united, and from them came the many dragons known today.

Nicole Petit writes because no other job lets her sleep until noon. Fantasy is her forte, a sliver of genre right between urban fantasy and fairy tales. She writes the *Magic Realm Manuscripts* series and has curated the collections *Just So Stories, After Avalon, and the award-winning From the Dragon Lord's Library series.*

Preview
The Curious Case of the Clockwork Doll
By Heidi J. Hewett

The thrilling January release in 18thWall Productions' The Science of Deduction

221b Baker Street has never lacked for visitors.

Princes and kings, washerwomen and governesses, the lost and the liars. But never one such as this.

But in the final days of the Boer War, Sherlock Holmes receives a most unexpected guest. A serving girl, whose clothes are ten years out of date and speaks in repeated phrases. She answers any question put to her with mathematical exactitude. More shocking is the secret hidden under her bonnet…

As Sherlock Holmes contends with this case, he must confront a master thief, a supposed ghost, uncommon butlers, miraculous engines Charles Babbage never dreamed of, and the impact of a war on the far side of the globe.

Chapter One

Among the many startling successes of Mr. Sherlock Holmes' career are a few unavoidable failures—not all of the cases presented to Holmes have resulted in a happy conclusion, as I observed in my account of *The Adventure of the Solitary Cyclist*. There have been occasions on which my friend exerted his great deductive powers of reasoning to unravel a mystery, and yet we arrived too late to prevent a tragedy.

I have noted that the period between 1894 and 1901 was one of the busiest for my friend, for he consulted in many public cases and hundreds of private cases of the most intricate and extraordinary character. Records of these cases, illustrating the curious problems presented to Mr. Holmes, are kept in the vaults of the bank of Cox and Co., but most have never been made known to the public.

One in particular concerned services to the crown which I was at the time unable to describe, being obliged as a partner and confidant to avoid any indiscretion. The whole affair was so carefully hushed up in the interests of national security that few, if any, know the events I am about to relate. But seeing that the South African war is long over, and it has been years since the Haviland name has been heard in England, it is perhaps as well that the true details of this inconceivable affair should now come to light.

The year was 1900. Holmes was, at the time, involved in the investigation of the theft of a rare and valuable artwork, a blackmail case, and the search for a washer-woman's lost brother, which, he said, was likely to prove the most interesting of the three. We were, however, only moderately engaged that particular morning, and Holmes, as usual, was dividing his time between his endless scrap-booking and the chemical experiments in which he took pleasure, while I reclined with my pipe in the old cane-backed chair in our little flat. The *Daily Telegraph* had slipped from my hands, and I was sitting, smoking meditatively, when my companion's voice interrupted the reverie into which I had fallen.

"Indeed, Watson," said he, still looking through the eyepiece of the microscope on the acid-stained, deal-topped table. "Of all of man's inventions, war is the most terrible. Pindar was right: there is a great difference between the idea and the fact."

I bolted upright in my chair in surprise. "But this is marvelous, Holmes! How could you have known what was in my thoughts just now?"

Holmes straightened and spun around on his stool. There was a mischievous twinkle in his eye. "I have demonstrated to you before that it is possible to read another's mind, if one has sufficient skill in observation."

"But how could you know I was thinking of that particular quote from Pindar?" I protested. "You have had your back turned to me, and I have been sitting here this entire time, with only my newspaper."

Holmes waved aside my objection. He crossed the room to the fireplace, and selecting a favorite long-stemmed pipe from the coal-scuttle, he began:

"The newspapers have been full of reports of the surrender of Pretoria in the Transvaal, and the expectation is that now that the capital has fallen, the war will soon be over—have you the tobacco-slipper? Ah! I see it next to you. If you would be so kind as to toss it to me. Thank you!—Yet earlier this morning you were telling me the Boers have taken up a defensive position in the hills. You speculated that our side could not afford to ignore the threat to rearward communications, and further action would be necessary."

Using the fire-tongs, he lit his pipe from a coal in the

grate and resumed:

"Just now, your old wound caused you momentary discomfort, and you thought back to the hardships which soldiers must endure: extremes of temperature, scarcity of food and supplies, fever, dysentery. In the reflection of the tea-pot, I observed you adjust your collar as if you felt warm and guessed that you were remembering your experiences among the Afghans.

"The futility of it—so many men sick and dying—struck you as you considered that Britain's interest in the region stems from an insatiable desire for diamonds and gold, which are plentiful in those parts, and your expression changed into one of disgust. It so happened then that a man passing in the street below chanced to whistle a phrase from the old war song, 'By Jingo,' and again you felt a patriotic stirring."

"I didn't even hear the man whistling!"

"Nevertheless, your mind took in the sensation. You sat up straighter in your chair. You remembered that Britain has an obligation to protect its colonists; that we have a moral duty to intervene on behalf of the black Africans whom the Boers enslave.

"Your eye chancing to fall upon an open book of Horace, you recalled his famous exhortation—for the undirected mind runs down habitual paths—that it is sweet and glorious to die for one's country. This quotation immediately put you in mind of another by Pindar: 'War is sweet to those who have never experienced it.' I then remarked that I heartily agreed with you and you were amazed." He blew out a cloud of smoke.

"So that was all there was to it!" I said, slapping my

thigh and laughing heartily. "Astonishing, Holmes! Why, you have laid the whole mystery bare, like the tumbler mechanism of a lock or the inner working of my pocket-watch! I thought at first there was something to it, but a child could see it now."

"Yes," said my friend with a note of bitterness, turning away. "The spectator is overcome with amazement when the magician pulls away the curtain to reveal the final result, but let him draw aside that curtain and show the steps by which that result is accomplished, and the spectator dismisses the achievement as nothing more than a cheap trick. So the chain of deductive reasoning laid out seems, retrospectively, a simple feat."

As my friend was speaking, I had shifted my position to the window-seat of our little flat, and happening to glance down into the street, I observed a lady heavily-veiled and dressed in black stepping out of a hansom cab.

Holmes joined me at the window. "It appears we have a client," he remarked, studying her through a parting in the curtain. "You see, she does not hesitate."

I saw her give the driver eight and sixpence without a word, and the hansom clattered away as she turned back to our door.

"The second half of a first class return ticket," Holmes said, snapping his magnifying lens shut and replacing it in his breast pocket. "The lady's clothes and carriage bespeak elegance, but her shoes are wrong. Someone who has been fairly well-to-do previously, but now lives within reduced circumstances. That bonnet, like an upside-down flower-pot, trimmed with a hideous assortment of feathers, hasn't been seen for ten years in London."

Just then, the lady in the street below glanced upward. Her eyes were hidden behind the veil, but she gazed so fixedly at the very spot where we stood that I was possessed by the uncomfortable sensation she had overheard our conversation.

I retreated from the window to stand behind the armchair.

"Now, Holmes, how could you possibly know about the fashion of ladies hats?"

Holmes let the curtain slip from his fingers. "It is my business to observe such small details. You remember the Abernetty case; everything of importance hinged on the parsley in the butter dish."

"She is clearly a woman of good character and birth," I said, recalling the graceful turn of the ankle as she stepped down from the hansom.

"I draw only such deductions as can be made from the evidence before me. She may be an axe murderer who has drowned babies and strangled cats."

"Holmes, you are a machine, an absolute machine! Have you no feeling at all?"

"It is a maxim of mine that women are never to be entirely trusted. The most winning woman of my acquaintance murdered three innocent children for their insurance-money. It is best not to let one's tender emotions cloud the superior function of the Intellect."

We heard the sharp clang of the bell, and a moment later our long-suffering housekeeper and landlady, Mrs. Hudson, gently rapped upon the door and announced, "There is a woman down below to see you, sir."

"A woman, and not a lady? Well, well! Ask her to step

up." Turning to me, Holmes continued, chuckling, "We shall see if we can detect what the excellent Mrs. Hudson has observed about our visitor."

There was a bustle outside on the landing, and Mrs. Hudson opened the door to usher in our guest.

She was, as I have mentioned, dressed in black silk under a traveling cloak, with an outmoded and unattractive hat. She wore black leather gloves, and her face was completely covered by a thick lace veil, so that it was difficult at first sight to say more than that she carried herself with dignity, and her voice, when she spoke, was exceedingly gentle and pleasant.

"Have I the honor of addressing, Mr. Sherlock Holmes?"

"And my associate, Doctor Watson," he said, waving in my direction and gesturing for her to take a seat. "There is nothing that can be said to me which cannot be said before him."

She turned toward me and inclined her head.

"And what brings you to London, Miss—?" my friend began, as I discreetly slipped out my pocket note-book.

"Haviland," said she. "My name is Martha Haviland."

"And you have a matter, Miss Haviland, on which you desire to consult me?"

"I have come on behalf of Miss Judith Haviland," she said. "She is the mistress of the Haviland estate. She would much value your advice regarding a succession of strange incidents that have occurred in connection with the house."

"I am all attention," said Holmes, casting himself into a chair and closing his eyes. "Pray give us the essential facts, and afterward I can question you as to any relevant details you may have missed."

"I will tell you what Miss Haviland wished me to tell you, that lately the family has been subject to the whims of an unseen force: capricious, sometimes malevolent. Small articles disappear or are discovered to have been moved. Drawers are opened. Some in the household report hearing noises in the passageways. Even at times, a cold touch has been felt." The veiled woman seated on the sofa fell silent, and I wondered who she was that she referred to Miss Haviland in this oblique way. Surely, I thought to myself, Mrs. Hudson must be mistaken. A poor relation of the Havilands, perhaps, but her speech and bearing suggested refinement of character and breeding.

"The family—" Holmes prompted. "Who lives in the house?"

"There is Miss Judith Haviland, Mr. Lionel Haviland, her brother, a nursery governess named Miss Berends, and her charge, Mary Haviland."

"And it is *Miss* Haviland to whom the property belongs?" I ventured. "That certainly is unusual."

The veiled woman made a curious yet graceful gesture, a half-circle of the wrist as if to say, *I cannot tell.*

"And the house?" Holmes questioned her. "Who else has access to the house? How is it situated?"

"We live a private, retired life," the woman said in her clear, measured voice. "The house in Sussex is remotely placed. We never see anyone except the occasional tradesman from the village."

"Then it is one of the servants," Holmes said, sitting up and opening his eyes without interest. "I suggest you recommend to Miss Haviland that she make a thorough inspection and give notice to the offender at once."

"One moment," I interjected, and the woman turned her head toward me. "You said, 'sometimes malevolent.'"

My friend had wandered to the mantelpiece and pulled down one of his reference books. "Haviland the inventor?" he asked over his shoulder.

The woman inclined her head.

"Has the ghost an identity?" I asked.

Again, the curious gesture of the wrist. "I do not know. Can you say more?"

"I have heard," I began cautiously, "that a ghostly visitation may betoken some unfinished business, even a cry for help."

"I am not aware. Can you say more?" she asked sweetly.

"Well," said I, becoming confused, "I mean to ask, does it have a name, this ghost? Is there any indication of its motive, why it is haunting this particular family or house?"

"I do not know. Can you say more?"

My friend interrupted in that brusque manner he sometimes chooses to adopt: "Good day, Miss Martha. Mrs. Hudson will see you out. You have had a long journey to London to no avail. I regret the trouble you have taken to see me," said he, turning his back and snapping the book shut.

The woman rose without a word and started toward the door, when, in one of those mercurial shifts of temper that characterized my friend, Holmes pivoted and called after her: "Do not go yet, Miss Martha. Please," he held out his hand, indicating her former seat. "There are one or two points in connection with your case not entirely devoid of interest. I beg you will continue."

"I have reported everything as Miss Haviland directed."

"Tell me, Miss Martha, how many miles is it from Eastbourne to London?" Holmes asked.

"73.2," was the prompt reply.

"And how many stops between Eastbourne and Victoria Station?"

"19."

"How much is 37,250 times 987?" A wild light was shining in Holmes' eyes and his tone had taken on a sportive, almost malicious quality.

She seemed about to speak, but stopped short, sensing a trap.

"As I was going to St. Ives, I met a man with seven wives," Holmes began to ramble to my astonishment:

"Each wife had seven sacks,

Each sack had seven cats,

Each cat had seven kits:

Kits, cats, sacks, and wives,

How many were there going to St. Ives?

"Oh, glorious! Glorious!" he concluded, crowing with sudden laughter. "No! Pray, don't go, Miss Martha. You are among friends!" He flapped his hands toward her in his excitement, urging her to make haste. "Pray, be uncovered! Pray, remove your veil."

Chapter Two

It was a face to rival the beauties of the day, with delicately formed lips, a small chin, high cheekbones, shapely brows, and large dark eyes hidden modestly behind lashes. Her countenance was at once child-like and womanly, of equal parts innocence and grace.

The skin was not like true skin, for Art cannot so perfectly replicate Nature, and I now understood why she wore gloves, else her hands should have given her away at once. The skin was without blemish, of a pale and rosy hue, and yet, I say, it filled me with revulsion and horror. She saw my look and paused in pinning up her veil. She turned her eyes full upon me then, and I saw that the aqueous orbs had the curiously flat quality of a being that possesses life, but no soul.

Holmes had crossed the room in a few quick steps and stood, hovering with barely contained excitement over the couch.

"You will permit...I am a student of Phrenology." Holmes carefully lifted the hat and set it aside. "The catch? Ah!" He exclaimed with a cry of satisfaction as it gave way.

Through a small square aperture we gazed down into Martha's brain. The horror of my previous impression was surpassed only by my wonder at what I beheld: a gelatinous blue sea encased in a bubble of glass finer and more fragile in appearance than that of an electrical bulb, in which floated a thousand sparks of light, rather say a thousand thousands, or more, for they were beyond numbering, like tiny signal ships winking to one another. Or perhaps it would be better to compare them to those strange, luminescent fish rumoured to live in the deepest part of the ocean, for the flashes did not merely float on the surface but appeared embedded in the blue jelly. Underneath, the dim outline of a small rectangular plate could be seen, from which a tangle of filaments descended, not unlike the nerves of a body. Some of the nerve filaments snaked away to microscopic metal discs embedded upon the inner surface of the outer visage, which was supported by a contoured scaffolding of tiny metal struts. Thicker cords of wires, twisted together like fibers of rope, fed into the brain from the eye and ear sockets.

"An automaton!" I exclaimed in breathless admiration.

"Most remarkable," Holmes murmured.

"I have never seen anything like it," I said. We both spoke in whispers. At each sound we uttered, flashes darted through the jelly, almost too quick for the human eye, momentarily lighting up a fantastical forest of miniature trees with a million forked branches and fading out of sight.

"But how did you know?" I asked.

"Descartes noted that by their nature, automata may appear to respond to stimuli, but are unable to produce variety of linguistic response, which simple questioning quickly reveals. You observed, no doubt, the repeated gestures and turns of phrase. I recognized the Haviland family name, which first set my thinking along these lines."

"Are you in any discomfort, Miss Martha?" I inquired.

"None," she replied, "I must return home before my electrical reserves are depleted."

I had heard of German and French experiments with batteries made of zinc and carbon, but this must have been something superior in sophistication. I glanced at the seated form, in so many respects identical to the genuine article, and wondered where her supply of power was housed. Did it replace the heart? One of the organs of digestion?

Holmes replaced the covering with a small sigh of regret. I think he would have liked to dissect her then and there if he had known where to start, but she was a creature far beyond either of our capabilities or experience.

"You may tell Miss Haviland," he said, addressing the automaton, "that we will take her case. I have one or two other cases at hand of some importance which require my presence in London, but she may expect us Wednesday next. A day in the country will do me no harm. Watson, I should be glad of your company, if you can spare the time."

I held the door open for her, and Miss Martha, for so I persisted in thinking of her, passed through, giving me a small, courteous nod, for all the world like a real woman of flesh and blood. It was so completely natural that I unthinkingly wished her good day. Closing the door, I turned and saw Holmes' smile.

"I dare say you thought I acted rather badly to Miss Martha just now?"

"I have learned to trust your judgment."

"Very sensible, Watson. And now as there is nothing more to be done, I shall devote myself to Hoffmann. If you would be so good as to consult Bradshaw near your elbow—I believe there is a train from Victoria at two o'clock—and ask Mrs. Hudson to send up dinner."

Holmes took up the violin from its case in the corner, and a few moments later the haunting notes of the barcarole could be heard throughout our apartment.

Holmes sat opposite me, for we had the first-class carriage to ourselves, and busied himself with *Le Figaro* as the train steamed southward. We had hardly passed Keymer Junction, however, before he cast it aside and sat drumming his fingers.

I looked up from the *Chronicle*. "Well, victory for our boys at Diamond Hill. The Boers will have no choice but to surrender to Roberts now, I think."

"Who?"

"Surely you are joking!" I exclaimed. "Field Marshal Frederick Roberts? Commander-in-Chief of the Forces? Why just the other day I was telling you about his capture of Pretoria. Those brave fellows are fighting for Britain out there. You might try to care."

"Crime is my business," my friend replied in his curt manner. "I am a brain, to which the rest of this," he gestured carelessly, "body, is mere appendage. The detection and unraveling of crime is my great purpose, toward which all my mental energies are devoted. I cannot afford to stuff my head with useless facts in the haphazard way you do, Watson."

I raised one eyebrow and retreated behind my newspaper.

Holmes continued to stare out the window over the landscape. We were still too far north on the line to see the Downs or the chalky cliffs of the coast, but the countryside was pleasant and dotted with small farms.

"Quite a change from the gloom of London, is it not, Watson?" Holmes mused gloomily. "Perhaps I shall one day withdraw into retirement. I will settle myself in some secluded spot like this and devote myself to the study of bees. Don't you miss it already? London? The great metropolis, riddled with factories and workshops. The docks swarming with trade from the far reaches of the Empire. Six million souls seething with activity as their individual ends direct them, fueling conflict and crime. There is food for the mind, exercise for one's talent!

"Well, well," he concluded sourly. "I shall investigate this paltry 'ghost' of the Havilands. There is quite enough ordinary evil to go around without invoking supernatural interference. But Martha," Holmes stopped and chuckled quietly to himself. "Martha interests me very much."

"It still fills me with wonder that such a thing is possible," I said. "How on earth did you work it out?"

"I recognized Haviland's name from my scrapbook in connection with a case I worked in '78—before your time, old fellow—for the French modeller, Tavernier. Haviland used to manufacture clockwork apparatus for him when his work called for it. I saw some of his early inventions, but nothing, nothing like this. I believe he has been dead now some five years.

"The estate belonged at one time to one of the wealthiest families in England, but mismanagement and neglect through successive generations reduced it to a shadow of its former self. In 1885 Haviland announced he was retiring from public life and retreated into this venerable wreckage of aristocratic poverty. The years passed. The great inventor produced nothing, and saw no one. His reputation crumbled, and it was whispered about that he had inherited the strain of insanity which runs in his family.

"I now believe that Arthur Haviland was, in fact, at work on his greatest invention of all—an invention so astounding it defies belief—and that his mania for secrecy prevented him from making it known. The Havilands are indeed a very private family, but I recall hearing that the son, Lionel, has, at a young age, learned to play heavily at cards and squander money on the turf."

While he was speaking, Holmes had taken out his pipe, which he laid across his knees, and he felt in his breast-pocket. "Perhaps that is the reason he has been disinherited in favor of the sister. Have you a match?"

I had not. "I'll go in search of the porter," said I and stepped out into the corridor. Before I had taken two strides, the connecting door at the far end of the carriage was flung open with great force, and a barrel-chested man with a cap pulled low over his eyes burst through, clutching a small case.

I stood my ground, prepared to block his progress, but he pulled down the window of the rushing train as it neared a bend in the track and flung the case down the embankment.

"Stop there!" I cried, and the man looked up at me. Just then, the conductor came through, shouting, "Thief!"

I heard the sharp, shrill sound of the brakes, and the train lurched to a stop.

Chapter Three

With a snarl the man pushed violently past me and disappeared through the connecting door behind me into the next car. I staggered to my feet as the conductor ran up.

"Are you all right, sir?"

"Fine, fine." I waved him on. "He threw a small case out that window."

The conductor stuck his head out of the window and looked back. The train had now come to a stop, just short of the Lewes Station. "I see it, sir." He took out his whistle and signaled to one of his fellows.

I returned to our compartment.

"There has been some excitement," I said. "Someone on this train appears to have been robbed. The thief must have panicked when the alarm was given and tossed the goods. I did my best to stop him, but the ruffian was too strong for me."

"You are unhurt?"

"Only my pride was injured," I explained ruefully.

"Well, well," Holmes said. "Hello! Here is a familiar face."

A moment later, the door to our compartment slid open, and Inspector Lestrade thrust his head inside.

"Ah, Mr. Holmes! I might have guessed you'd be mixed up in this business."

Holmes had sunk back against the cushions, and he surveyed the Scotland Yard detective with a languid, half-smile. "I assure you I am perfectly innocent of any involvement. Pray, enlighten me."

Lestrade's ferret-like eyes narrowed. "You mean you're

not here on the trail of Jack of Diamonds?"

"Certainly not. I have been engaged by a client in the vicinity of Fulworth on an entirely separate matter. What is this Jack of Diamonds supposed to have done?"

Lestrade's manner changed entirely. "Well, then, Mr. Holmes. Seeing as you're here, and that you have been of assistance to us on the Force once or twice before...."

I coughed.

Holmes modestly waved Lestrade's understatement aside and indicated that the inspector should be seated.

Lestrade took off his hat and sat down. "We had an anonymous tip there might be a robbery on this line."

"Watson here saw the thief," Holmes said.

Lestrade turned to me with interest. "Did you now? And do you think you could describe him?"

"Well," I said hesitantly as Lestrade pulled out his note-book. "It was only a brief moment, but I should say he was middle-size, a strongly built man. Rather a thick neck, square jaw, moustache."

"Square jaw, moustache. Right." Lestrade tapped his pencil against the page.

Holmes chuckled. "Why, my dear Watson, you have just described half the men in England. Middle-size? A moustache?"

"A disguise?"

"Undoubtedly."

"Disguise or no disguise, we'll catch him. We have him dead to rights this time," Lestrade said with grim triumph. "The lady's maid raised the alarm as soon as she saw the jewel case was missing. The conductor says he happened to notice a furtive-looking man and followed him. When he called out to him to stop, the thief broke into a run, but the conductor says, except when his view was blocked between the carriages, he had him in sight. My men are going through the train now. It's a matter of time before we identify him."

"I should advise then that you look for a man without a moustache," Holmes said.

"He can't hide forever," Lestrade said. "He's on this train. We've got him and the jewels this time."

"Excuse me, sir." A plainclothes detective, sweating profusely, tapped on the glass and entered our compartment, bearing a small, black case.

"That's the one," I said, pointing to it.

Holmes suppressed a smile. "Your ability to identify a carrying case is somewhat better than your ability to identify the man who took it."

"We've searched the train," the plainclothes man said. "We found this down the embankment."

Lestrade was wrestling with the case. "It's locked."

"Here, sir. Lady Kildaire gave me the key."

Lestrade inserted the key and turned it in the lock. The case opened with a snap.

"He's done it again," Lestrade growled, tossing the jewel case onto the seat beside him.

I looked into the velvet folds of the interior. The case was empty.

Holmes bent forward to pick up the red and white playing card that had drifted to the floor and turned it over in his hands. "The Jack of Diamonds. Our mysterious friend has also been busy on the Continent," Holmes remarked. "Vienna last month. Paris before that. Prague two weeks ago. I recognized the *modus operandi* at once."

"You've been following this case?" I asked.

"Only incidentally. I read the papers, my dear Watson, just as you do, but to greater purpose."

"I'm surprised you haven't taken more of an interest in this business," said Lestrade.

Holmes shrugged. "As the poet says, *'Who steals my purse steals trash; 'tis something, nothing; 'Twas mine, 'tis his...'* Every jewel of real value has a long and bloody history. And Lady Kildaire is not my client. Still, the solution is obvious, is it not?"

"Oh, so you've solved the case already, have you?" Lestrade said bitterly.

"I have told you it is not my affair."

"Wait," I interjected. "I think I have it. What if there were two cases.... This Jack fellow steals one and passes it to his accomplice on the train, who substitutes a second, empty case, which Jack then tosses out the window?"

"No, no," Lestrade interrupted. "Say Jack grabs the goods, tosses them out the window. Then his accomplice nabs the real jewel case and substitutes this one in its place before we can arrive on the scene."

Holmes steepled together his long, thin fingers. "I can assure you, gentlemen, there is only one jewel case in this affair, and this is that case."

"Impossible," said Lestrade. "We know he couldn't have removed the jewels from the case before throwing it from the train, and there wasn't time enough for him, or his accomplice, to pick the lock, remove the jewels, and substitute his playing card unobserved, before Symmonds climbed down the embankment."

Holmes sat forward suddenly. "The train has started."

"The constables at Lewes are waiting for us. We can conduct a full search of all the passengers on the train at the station," Lestrade said.

Holmes laughed, "Of course!"

Lestrade was stung. "You have your clever ways of knowing things, Mr. Holmes, but sometimes it comes down to manpower in cases like these." The train had rolled forward and come to rest in the station with a hiss of steam and scream of the brakes. Lestrade rose to his feet.

"The jewels never left London," Holmes said.

"You mean this is all a hoax?" Lestrade demanded. "An insurance scam?"

"No, the robbery is genuine, but it occurred before Lady Kildaire ever boarded the train. This whole case-snatching was just for show, to make it appear the robbery had only just occurred."

"But why draw attention to it at all?" I asked. "Why not simply take the jewels and no one the wiser?"

"Someone is always bound to notice when a set of valuables goes missing. But *when* it was taken has a way of obscuring *who* took it."

"Is that so?" Lestrade said. "I don't suppose you have any further information you'd like to share that would put us on the track of this Jack of Diamonds character?"

"As to that," said Holmes, "I expect he is long gone. Most likely he left the train as soon as we pulled into Lewes, possibly disguised as a signalman or a constable. You'll have better luck arresting his accomplice."

"His accomplice?" Lestrade objected. "You said his throwing the case from the train was nothing but a false scent to take us off his trail!"

"Unless I am mistaken, you will find Lady Kildaire's maid most willing to assist you in your investigation after she discovers she has lost both her lover and the fortune in jewels he promised her. Poor girl. Still, it's not a hanging offense, is it?"

Preview
The Door of Eternal Night
By Josh Reynolds

The horrifying February release in 18thWall Productions'
The Science of Deduction

In the heady days of the Jazz Age, Sherlock Holmes has retired to his bees. But other, stranger detectives watch London in his absence.

Chief among them is Charles St. Cyprian, the current Royal Occultist and heir to a tradition reaching back to Elizabethan England. He, along with his apprentice Ebe Gallowglass, protect the Empire and sundry from That Which Man Was Not Meant to Know—including vampires, ghosts, werewolves, ogres, fairies, boggarts and the occasional worm of unusual size.

Tonight, St. Cyprian's night out has been interrupted by two very important men, Harry Houdini and Sir Arthur Conan Doyle. The escapist and spook-buster has a problem–a spook haunting his hotel room, a spook he can't quite bust. And it seems this particularly ghost has a baring on a case Sherlock Holmes failed to solve, and may solve yet, if St. Cyprian doesn't untangle the mystery first.

CHAPTER ONE

THE KNIGHT AND THE MAGICIAN

"It was all a dream, of course. Or so I thought, at the

time," Harry Houdini said, as he finished his story. "What else could it be?" He sat back in his chair, crossing his legs. "Anyway, I apologize for disturbing you, Mr. St. Cyprian—but Arthur was damn insistent."

Houdini gestured to the big, elderly man who sat perched on the edge of the nearby Chesterfield, his thick fingers knotted together. He had a large, bushy moustache and kindly eyes, which were nonetheless brimming with exasperation. "And with good reason, whatever you might think, Harry," Sir Arthur Conan Doyle rumbled. "But Mr. St. Cyprian is the expert—why not let him come to his own conclusions?"

In contrast to the angular Houdini and the hearty Conan Doyle, Charles St. Cyprian was a slim man of olive complexion dressed in one of the finest modern sartorial creations to ever emerge from the depths of a Savile Row tailors' shop. He had been preparing for a long-overdue evening out when his guests had arrived and insisted on speaking, despite the lack of appointment. But when an internationally recognized stage magician and the biographer of the world's foremost consulting detective showed up at one's doorstep, demanding attention, one had best brew a cuppa or three and settle in for a chat, regardless of social niceties.

St. Cyprian took a sip of his tea and said, "Thank you, Sir Arthur. Might I ask what makes you think it was a dream, Mr. Houdini?"

"Call me Harry. And because I don't believe in spooks, Mr. St. Cyprian," Houdini said. "But I believe in fools who do, no offense, Arthur."

Conan Doyle frowned. "None taken, Harry."

116

Houdini smiled thinly. "He's a bad liar, isn't he?" He slapped his knees. "It's a trick, plain and simple. Someone's having a chuckle at my expense—well, I won't stand for it. I've never yet been rooked by a phony spirit, and I don't intend to start now."

"No, well, we wouldn't want that, would we?" St. Cyprian put aside his cup and saucer. He glanced at Conan Doyle. "You disagree, Sir Arthur?"

"Most certainly," Conan Doyle said, stiffly. "I know psychic phenomena when I see it, sir. Indeed, I have seen much that science would be hard-pressed to explain. What of that Australian fellow, a psychometrist of some note, who traced the whereabouts of a missing man after touching his boot? Police forces in Europe and America call in specialists on baffling cases regularly." He leaned forward and tapped the side of his nose. "Indeed, I'm planning a trip to Australia and New Zealand in a few months to speak on that very matter."

"Of course you are," Houdini said.

Conan Doyle glared at him. "One day, Harry, I will make you see that the world is not simply a puzzle to be solved. Your own abilities..."

"Tricks, Arthur. Hokum. Legerdemain." Houdini gestured sharply. "I keep telling you—why don't you believe me?"

Conan Doyle fell silent, and St. Cyprian felt a moment of sympathy for the great man. Sir Arthur had lost a child in the War, as had countless others. And like many, he had turned to spiritualism, seeking comfort from and explanation for that grievous loss. St. Cyprian knew better than most that there were precious few answers to be found from the dead...only more questions, or worse. And sometimes, it was best for all concerned if those questions never came to light. Such was the responsibility of the Royal Occultist.

Formed during the reign of Elizabeth the First, the office of Royal Occultist was charged with the investigation, organization and occasional suppression of That Which Man Was Not Meant to Know—including vampires, ghosts, werewolves, ogres, fairies, boggarts and the occasional worm of unusual size—by order of the King (or Queen), for the good of the British Empire. Beginning with the diligent amateur Dr. John Dee, the office had passed through a succession of hands, some worthy, some otherwise, culminating, for the moment, in the year 1920 with one Charles St. Cyprian. He leaned forward.

"If you would be so kind, talk me through it again, Mr. Houdini—Harry," he asked. As he spoke, he idly clinked together the trio of strange rings that adorned his fingers. Each of the rings was inscribed with a series of characters that might have been Cyrillic or Hebrew or something else entirely. He wasn't entirely sure what they did, even now, but every Royal Occultist since Dee had worn them and it seemed less than wise to break with the tradition.

"Why? So you can convince me nothing is something?" Houdini said. "Look at this place." He gestured airily to their surroundings. The house at 427 Cheyne Walk was a perk of the job and had been since the Regency. Placed perfectly on Victoria Embankment to watch over certain old structures long hidden by the Thames, the house was unassuming, blending perfectly with its surroundings, at least from the outside. Inside, pictures of former bearers of the office lined the walls of the sitting room, jostling for space with fetish masks and lurid artworks by Goya and Blake. Great bookshelves groaned beneath a library of occult works, as well as a century's worth of accumulated bric-a-brac. On the mantle of the large, Restoration era fireplace, grisly statuary glared morosely at the visitors.

"Whatever your title, you're as bad as Arthur."

"Technically, I'm a good bit worse," St. Cyprian said. "Humor me, if you would."

Houdini sighed theatrically. "It's your dime." He spread his hands. "Mrs. Houdini and I—my wife, Wilhelmina, I mean—are staying at Claridge's. You know it?"

"I've had the pleasure of Mr. Carte's hospitality, yes," St. Cyprian said.

Houdini nodded. "Swanky joint, if you can afford it. Anyway, Mrs. Houdini and I were getting ready for bed, when I felt something." He paused. "You ever get the creeps, Mr. St. Cyprian?"

"Charles, please. And yes, quite often."

Houdini smiled. "I bet you do, living in a place like this, Charley."

St. Cyprian raised an eyebrow at the familiarity, but said nothing. Houdini was a showman—he liked getting a rise out of people, one way or another. "You felt something," he said. "A change in temperature, perhaps?"

"Yeah. Pretty standard, when someone's trying to fake a phantom. Ice under the floorboards, crack in a window, that sort of thing."

"But not in this case," St. Cyprian said.

Houdini frowned. "I'll figure it out."

"Only a fool distrusts the evidence of his own senses,"

Conan Doyle said. "Especially senses like yours, Harry."

"Flattery aside, senses are easy to fool. That's practically my bread and butter, Arthur," Houdini said, rolling his eyes.

"Exactly!" Conan Doyle slapped his knee. "And who better to know if he was being fooled. That you can't, implies that you aren't."

"Or that it's a new, more subtle form of trick," St. Cyprian murmured.

Houdini gestured. "See? Even your ghost-breaker pal agrees with me!"

Before Conan Doyle could argue further, St. Cyprian said, "I neither agree nor disagree. In my experience, things are rarely what they seem. Further investigation is called for. What happened next?"

Houdini was silent for a moment. Then, at a nudge from Conan Doyle, he said, "I saw a guy...a real swell gent. Old fashioned though. Worse than Arthur here."

"I beg your pardon," Conan Doyle blustered.

"Apology accepted," Houdini said. "Didn't look like a spook. More like a banker. Only..." he hesitated again.

St. Cyprian sat back. He fished a silver cigarette case out of his jacket and popped it open. He took one of the hand-rolled cigarettes out and popped it into his mouth while he waited for Houdini to finish. "Only what?" he pressed, as he proffered the case to his guests.

"Hand-rolled. An oriental blend?" Conan Doyle said, waving the offer aside. Houdini shook his head, frowning.

"A Moro woman of my acquaintance," St. Cyprian said, as he slid the case back in his jacket. He touched an index finger to the tip of the cigarette, and puffed gently. A thin tendril of smoke rose as he shook his finger. Houdini glared at him.

"That supposed to impress me, Charley?"

"Is what supposed to impress you?" St. Cyprian said. "Now...you were saying? What about this banker so perturbed you?"

"Besides the fact that he was in my room in the middle of the night?"

"Besides that, yes," St. Cyprian said, smiling slightly.

"He was...missing something." Houdini tapped his chest. "Didn't look like he gave it up willingly either." He swallowed. "It was red. Like it was on fire, and I could see..." He trailed off. "I could see everything that wasn't there," he said, finally.

St. Cyprian took a drag on his cigarette. "And then?"

"He said something. Only I couldn't make it out. It was like he was under water, or far away. It was just noise. Then he was gone." Houdini snapped his fingers. "Like a soap bubble popping. Damndest thing." He shook his head. "I'd pay good money to know how it was done. I could use a trick like that in my act."

"Unless it wasn't a trick," Conan Doyle said.

They began to bicker again, and St. Cyprian excused himself. He stood and wandered towards the fireplace, thinking. It could have been a trick. He'd seen such before, and Houdini was a ripe target for such a ploy—the famous medium-buster, busted at last. It would garner headlines, if nothing else. Houdini would be ruined, or, at least severely embarrassed. Spiritualists and seers the world over would sigh in relief.

"But it doesn't feel like a trick," he murmured, watching

the fire.

"Holmes used to talk to himself. He said it was the only way he could be certain of a good conversation," Conan Doyle said. St. Cyprian turned. The other man stood behind him, hands clasped behind his back. Houdini still sat in his chair, frowning at nothing in particular. Their arguments were quick things, brief spurts of heat, quickly snuffed.

"Did you ever take offense?"

"What would have been the point?" Conan Doyle said, with a shrug. "Watson endured more than I ever did. He had to live with him, after all." He paused. Then, "I...was sorry to hear about Thomas. He was a good man. Much like my own...my Kingsley."

"Yes," St. Cyprian said, stirring the fire with the poker.

"Did you ever...I mean, I know you and Carnacki were all over, but, did you..." Conan Doyle began, hesitantly.

"We never had the pleasure, no," St. Cyprian said. "I'm sorry."

Conan Doyle waved a hand. "Do not apologize." He looked at Houdini. "In any event, we are not here to reminisce about a life lost, but to save another."

"You think this spirit means Houdini harm, then?"

"Quite the contrary—I think it was attempting to warn him," Conan Doyle said fervently.

"Your chum Holmes ran across something similar in late 1899 or thereabouts," St. Cyprian said, scratching his chin. "Carnacki was just starting out, then. Holmes approached him during an investigation...something to do with a chap named Phillimore and a brolly?"

Conan Doyle nodded vigorously. "I remember that. Watson spoke of it once or twice. The tale of Mr. James

122

Phillimore, who, stepping back into his house to get his umbrella, was never more seen in this world," he said, with an air of recitation. He shook his head. "John claimed to have written about it, but it's still locked up tight in that tin dispatch box of his, so I've never seen it."

St. Cyprian nodded. "I only know some of it. Supposedly Phillimore, like our Mr. Houdini, had the misfortune to meet a ghostly harbinger...unfortunately, its warnings fell on deaf ears. Or simply came too late. Phillimore was gone a few days later, never to be seen again." He continued to stir the fire, thinking.

"Holmes never spoke of a ghost," Conan Doyle said.

"No, I rather think he wouldn't have. Holmes was convinced that it was trick and Thomas already had a reputation, much like Mr. Houdini's, for outing fraudulent mystics." St. Cyprian stepped back, frowning slightly, the poker resting on his shoulder. "They never figured it out. Or so Thomas claimed. A few months later, Holmes became preoccupied with another case—some beastly business in Ipswich—and Thomas took up his duties as Edwin Drood's apprentice." He heard the door slam. "And speaking of apprentices..."

"I got him," a young woman's voice crowed. "Right where you said he'd be, too. Cheeky bugger. Had to hit him with a—oh. Guests, is it?" she said, as she came into the sitting room, dragging a heavy roll of purple cloth. Somewhere, a church was missing its altar cloth, St. Cyprian suspected.

The newcomer was dark and slightly feral looking, with black hair cut in a razor-edged bob and a battered flat cap resting high on her head. She wore a man's clothes, hemmed for a woman of her small stature, beneath a heavy convoy coat that had seen better decades. There was something dark splattered on both the coat and her trousers, and she'd tracked more of whatever it was in across the floor. Conan Doyle and Houdini stared at her, and she stared back.

She let the roll of cloth flop heavily to the floor. There was something unpleasant wrapped in its stained folds, and it groaned softly, until Gallowglass gave it a swift kick. "Should have figured we had guests, if you were still here." She grinned at St. Cyprian. "What'd she say when you begged off, then?"

"What did who say?" St. Cyprian said.

"Whichever dolly-bird you were seeing tonight.' She looked at Houdini and Conan Doyle. "Sometimes they throw things at him. One of them sent him a scorpion in the post once."

"I say...a real one?" Conan Doyle said. He looked at St. Cyprian speculatively.

"Gentlemen, my apprentice, Miss Ebe Gallowglass. Late of Cairo, currently of Kensington. Miss Gallowglass, may I introduce Sir Arthur Conan Doyle and his good friend, Mr. Harry Houdini?" St. Cyprian said quickly.

"Ey up," Gallowglass said. She shot St. Cyprian a look. "I'm his assistant."

"That's what I said," St. Cyprian protested.

"What's in the bag?" Houdini said.

Gallowglass shrugged. "Bogey."

"A bogey?" Conan Doyle said, eyes wide. He seemed to have forgotten about the scorpion, thankfully.

"What's a bogey?" Houdini said.

124

"It's what's in the bag," Gallowglass said, pushing her cap back up on her head. She looked at St. Cyprian. "Want me to...*kchkk*?" She drew her thumb across her throat.

'No. Put him in that devil-box we brought back from Lewes last month. I daresay that'll keep the perisher quiet until we can figure out what to do with him," St. Cyprian said. "And then come back down. We have work to do."

"Joy," Gallowglass said. She grabbed the edges of the cloth and began to drag it towards the stairs. St. Cyprian winced each time whatever was inside bumped on the steps. He looked apologetically at his guests.

"She's really quite handy."

"A modern woman, by the looks of her," Conan Doyle said.

"Was she dragging a man up the stairs?" Houdini said. "I could swear I heard that carpet groan." He stared after Gallowglass, his expression puzzled and a bit apprehensive.

"Not a man, no," St. Cyprian said. "An unwelcome tenant, soon to be transported elsewhere. I'd like to see your room, if I might. At Claridge's, I mean."

"I've already checked it," Houdini said, still looking at the stairs.

"Nonetheless," St. Cyprian said. He tossed the remains of his cigarette into the fireplace. "Think of it as a second opinion, if you will. A fresh set of eyes."

Houdini traded glances with Conan Doyle, and sighed. "Fine. Like I said, it's your dime, Charley. It's your dime."

"Excellent!" St. Cyprian said. He rubbed his hands together in glee. "Now, let's go have a chat with this ghost of yours."

CHAPTER TWO

Mrs. Houdini

Claridge's sat snugly at the corner of Brook Street and Davies Street, in Mayfair. The hotel had flourished in the wake of the War as displaced aristocrats of all nationalities sought a suitable London residence. Supposedly, the deposed and exceedingly maudlin king of Ruritania lived at Claridge's when he wasn't serving as the doorman at Barribault's.

"Swanky sort of place, innit," Ebe Gallowglass said, as they followed Houdini and Conan Doyle inside. The foyer was a thing of columns and a floor of alternating black and white tiles. A chandelier hung at its centre and there was a curving set of stairs to their right. "Nicer than the Savoy. Wonder if they got a beastie in the basement as well."

"I shouldn't think so. And I'll ask you to be on your best behaviour, Miss Gallowglass," St. Cyprian said. "No raiding the bar, no threatening the guests, no unlimbering that artillery piece you call a pistol, *if you please.*"

"What—this?" Gallowglass said, pulling back the edge of her coat to reveal the heavy shape of the Webley-Fosbery revolver holstered beneath her arm. "Self-defense, innit?"

"I doubt we're going to be attacked by anything more dangerous than snide commentary in here, so hands off," he said firmly. His assistant had the distressing habit of seeing problems as a nail, and herself as a hammer. It was one he was trying his damndest to break her of.

If she lived long enough, Gallowglass would have his job, and be welcome to it, given that he'd likely be dead. Few Royal Occultists lived to collect a pension, though more than one had defied the odds to die alone, unsung, and unremembered at an unseemly age in a debtor's prison or a hospice ward. He liked to think he'd make it long enough to write his memoirs, but he doubted it. There was a reason Carnacki had allowed that fellow Dodgson—or was it Hodgson?—to write about him for *The Idler*, after all.

Perhaps that was why the Great Detective had allowed Conan Doyle to record his cases. St. Cyprian wondered whether the man had been slyly pleased at the publicity, even as he made a show of disdaining it. Perhaps Holmes had been, at heart, a showman, much like Houdini. *Too bad I can't ask him*. Holmes had, by all accounts, retired to Sussex at the end of the War, to enjoy his dotage and bees.

Thinking of Holmes made him recall the case of James Phillimore. Carnacki had been assiduous about keeping records. Dodgson's stories had been sanitized for public consumption, either by the writer or Carnacki himself. But the records told the unvarnished truth. Somewhere in the dozens of moleskin notebooks which littered the desk in his study was a record of the events pertaining to that case. As he and the others followed Houdini up the stairs, St. Cyprian wondered if he should dig the notes on the Phillimore case out.

The Houdinis had taken a suite on the third floor, with windows looking out over Brook Street, and the rows of terraced houses which lined it. Houdini didn't bother to knock, before flinging the door wide, to reveal a large sitting room, occupied by couches, chairs, and a fine piano which sat opposite a modest fireplace. Sumptuous rugs were spread protectively across the hardwood floors, and a small chandelier hung over the centre of the room.

St. Cyprian stopped as he came in, senses prickling. He cast a quick glance around, but saw nothing. Nonetheless, he felt it. There was something here, and yet...not. He could almost hear it. Like the hiss of a Victrola with its needle askew. His palms were suddenly sweaty. He felt Conan Doyle grip his elbow. "You feel something, don't you Charles?"

"Something, yes. I can't say exactly what, however."

"I've returned, sweetheart mine," Houdini said, throwing out his arms and puffing his chest. "Come and greet our guests, Mrs. Houdini." A thin, seemingly frail woman ducked under his arm and took Conan Doyle's hands.

"Arthur, you dear man. It's been ages," she said, ignoring Houdini.

Conan Doyle laughed and bent so that she could kiss his cheek. "Mrs. Houdini, as ever you are the light in the darkness."

"And what am I? Chopped liver?" Houdini protested.

"Wilhelmina, but you can call me Bess," Mrs. Houdini said, extending a pale hand towards St. Cyprian. "I don't believe we've been introduced. Are you a friend of Arthur's? He said he was taking Mr. Houdini to meet a spiritualist of some sort, only you don't look like a fraud at all."

"Bess," Houdini said, almost plaintively.

"Looks can be deceiving," Gallowglass said, pushing

129

past St. Cyprian. Hands in her pockets, she slouched towards the suite's liquor cabinet. A bottle of something red was already out, and sampled. "Who wants a drink?"

Bess watched the young woman pounce on the potables, and then glanced at her husband. "Have we adopted an alley cat, Mr. Houdini?"

"Mine, I'm afraid. I apologize for Miss Gallowglass' lack of social graces. Her talents lie in stranger vales than that of politesse. And I am Charles St. Cyprian. Neither spiritualist, nor fraud, though I know a bit about both."

"A pleasure to meet you, Mr. St. Cyprian. Arthur says you're the man to see about ghosts and such," Mrs. Houdini said. She smiled as she said it. From what he'd read, Bess Houdini was no less a sceptic than her husband, albeit a more genial one. For Houdini, it was a war. For Mrs. Houdini, it was a minor disagreement.

"I am indeed," St. Cyprian said. "Would you mind showing us where the spectre in question made its appearance?"

"Right to it, then?" Mrs. Houdini said, bemused. "I thought you English-types liked small talk."

"Ordinarily, I would be at your disposal, but your husband seemed most insistent that we get this over and done with as quickly as possible."

"Like I said on the way over, Charley...we've got a show tonight, for a private audience. They want to see the Great Houdini up close and personal. Who am I to deny them such a rare opportunity?" Houdini said. He pointed. "It was in the bedroom. Mrs. Houdini?"

"Follow me," Bess said.

She led them to a large bedroom, which was set off to

the side of the sitting room. Its windows were on the same side, and he could see the glow of the street lights through them. A large four-poster bed occupied most of the space, and a rolled up carpet leaned against one wall.

"I checked every inch of this room after our guest vanished," Houdini said, leaning against the door frame. "No hidden wire, no holes in the ceiling, walls, or floor. I was tempted to peel the wallpaper, but I'm already spending enough dough on this joint without adding a bill for damages in."

The sensation St. Cyprian had felt upon entering the suite was stronger here. It emanated from nowhere in particular, or perhaps everywhere. Something from Outside had come in, and it still had its foot in the door. There was a sort of miasma to these things, a creeping odour of the intangible. He traded a glance with Gallowglass, who nodded.

"Yeah," she said. She felt it as well.

He gestured, and she nodded. She sank to her haunches near the bed and extracted a mouldering satchel from her coat pocket. Strange sigils were stitched onto the satchel. She plucked a piece of chalk from it.

"You want to do the honours, or you want me to do it?" she asked, bouncing the satchel on her palm.

"You're the one with the artist's touch. Keep it neat, though. Remember what happened in Lewes, what?"

"That wasn't my fault," Gallowglass said sourly. "The floor were wonky." She extracted several short sections of polished wood and began to assemble them into something resembling a snooker cue. Once it was complete, she attached the chalk to the tip and began to scratch out a circle around them. As she did so, she murmured the words to a certain incantation, crafted by Dr. Dee himself for situations such as these.

While Gallowglass drew the protective pentacle, St. Cyprian reached into his coat pocket, feeling through the various amulets and charms which he carried with him at all times. One never knew when one might need an Assyrian demon-whistle, or a silver coin blessed by the Anti-Pope of Avignon, and it was best to have them close to hand, just in case. His fingers closed on the bottle of Hyssop oil, and he extracted it, giving it a deft shake as he did so.

"Medicine oil?" Houdini said, as he eyed the vial.

"Hyssop," Conan Doyle said, confidently. "A purifying agent."

"Very observant, Sir Arthur," St. Cyprian said as, thumb over the top of the vial, he began to sprinkle the oil around the interior of the circle. "It can also be used to protect those seeking to commune with the spirits."

"Bushwa," Houdini coughed into his fist.

St. Cyprian smiled serenely. "Quite possibly. I do know it's more effective on some occasions than others. Ghosts are rather like a...spiritual fungus, if you will. Some of them are more resistant than your average spook."

"Spiritual fungus," Houdini repeated. "Far cry from the usual line, I admit. What do you think, Arthur? Still backing your boy's play?"

"Despite the inelegance of the description, I have no argument with it," Conan Doyle said stiffly. Mrs. Houdini laid a hand on his arm and frowned at her husband.

"Mr. Houdini, I'll ask you to stop baiting poor Sir

Arthur. He's trying to help, as you well know." She smiled prettily at Houdini. "And since you seem stumped, what say we let them give it a try, hunh?"

"Spiritual fungus," Houdini said again, as if that answered her question.

"If I'm not mistaken, you admitted to believing in psychic phenomena of some kinds, didn't you, Mr. Houdini?" St. Cyprian said, not looking at the magician.

"I thought I asked you to call me Harry?"

"Forgive me," St. Cyprian said. "Harry then— telekinesis, ectoplasm, that sort of thing?"

"I offered cash for proof, if that's what you're getting at," Houdini said. "Maybe there's something there, maybe not, but I've yet to see any evidence."

St. Cyprian said nothing. If Houdini wanted proof, he could stick around. Then, some minds were like fortresses. Nothing of the spirit world could penetrate their psychic defences, or not permanently at any rate. Mostly they saw nothing at all, and what they did see, they soon forgot or rationalized. Houdini was the latter sort, he suspected. His mental equilibrium was enviable, as was his spiritual fortitude.

Gallowglass was of a similar cut. There was something about her which put off the more ethereal types, St. Cyprian had noticed. In the same way dockside roughs would cross to the other side of the street when they saw her coming towards them, ghosts, spooks and spectres would waft out of her path with unseemly haste. She rarely appeared to notice them, and when she did, she mostly ignored them, unless they were a threat.

"Will you be calling the ghost tonight?" Conan Doyle

said, breaking the moment of silence. "Are the aetheric vibrations conducive to such an attempt?"

St. Cyprian hesitated. He traded looks with Gallowglass, licked his finger and held it up. After a moment, he said, "Yes."

Conan Doyle flushed as Houdini laughed. "Are you mocking me, sir?"

"Heaven forefend, Sir Arthur. The truth of it is that ghosts have a sort of...of frequency, I guess you could say. Once they've made an appearance, all it takes is a bit of fiddling with the knob to bring them back. Quiet you," he added, as Gallowglass snickered. "Tonight would be best. The closer to the moment of its initial appearance, the stronger the signal."

"This gets better and better," Houdini said.

"Has he told you about the Thin Man yet?" Mrs. Houdini said, mildly, as she watched them make their preparations. Houdini stared at her in chagrin. She ignored him. "That gentleman who chased our car from the train station? The one who was watching us from across the street as we dined last night?"

"No, I daresay he didn't," St. Cyprian said, looking up at the magician.

"Harry—what is this? What's she talking about?" Conan Doyle said.

"It's nothing, Arthur. We get creeps like that all the time. Don't we, Mrs. Houdini?"

"No," she said, with evident good humour.

"I'm shocked, Mrs. Houdini. Shocked and appalled," Houdini protested.

"Mrs. Houdini," St. Cyprian began.

"Bess, please, Charles," Bess said, smiling at him.

St. Cyprian inclined his head. "Bess, then. Why do you call him the Thin Man?"

"Obvious reason, really. He's a bit of nothing, stretched out and fluffed up. Strange sort—haven't seen robes like that since Cairo. Taller than any Egyptian, though. Too tall, really." She hesitated. "I don't like him. He's been shadowing us since we got to London. Almost as if he's keeping an eye on us for some reason."

"Why didn't you tell me about this, Harry?" Conan Doyle said.

Houdini threw up his hands. "Why? We go through this in every town. If it's not Arabs throwing me down a hole, it's German spies trying to seal me in Bakelite. I'm famous, Arthur—there's a downside to it, as you well know." He glared at them. "Look, I got this show to do. Mrs. Houdini?"

"Everything's sorted. A motor car will be here to pick us up in a few minutes. I've got your bag, a few tricks suitable for a party—your handcuffs, that sort of thing. Gave the stage crew a night off as well, but told them to be back at the theatre at nine. Colonel Bobdillo is taking us out for dinner first, and then..."

"Bobdillo?" Conan Doyle said.

"You know him?" Houdini asked.

"I don't believe so, no. But I've heard the name perhaps. Dashed if I can remember where though," Conan Doyle said, doubtfully. Though he said nothing, St. Cyprian felt an inkling of the familiar as well...a snatch of memory, but in regards to what he couldn't say.

He rolled the name over in his head as he continued his

preparations. Something to do with Carnacki, perhaps? London was lousy with occultist of various stripes. Most were of the harmless variety—little more than antiquarians of a ghoulish bent. He knew most of them, by name at least. It paid to have a list of who'd bought what, when it came to certain outré items. He'd headed off a fair few problems that way.

Before he could say anything, someone knocked at the door to the suite. A few moments later, Houdini ushered a small, straight figure into the suite. "What are the odds? The man himself," Houdini said as the newcomer bobbed into the bedroom and turned.

"I'll allow as how my ears were burning, yes. Allow me to introduce myself—Colonel Bobdillo, Jasper to my friends, among which I hope you'll be counted," the little man said, as he took Mrs. Houdini's hand and patted it in a grandfatherly manner. His voice was a wheezy hiss. He wore a frayed overcoat, long out of fashion, and a top hat that added considerably to his meagre height. "I am most pleased to meet you, Mr. Houdini. I have long been an admirer of your exploits in the field of amateur escapology. When I saw that you would be coming once more to our fair shores, I thought it surely destiny." He glanced around, head wobbling.

Houdini preened. "Well, who am I to argue with destiny? Shall we get this show on the road? Arthur—care to join us?" He glanced at Bobdillo. "I'm sure the Colonel doesn't mind if the esteemed Sir Arthur Conan Doyle tags along."

"Mind? No, great heavens, no. The eminent author himself? The great defender of Spiritualism? Why, we'd be honoured. But what about your other friends? I don't believe that we've been introduced yet, sir," Colonel Bobdillo said, as St. Cyprian stood.

"St. Cyprian. Charles St. Cyprian," St. Cyprian said. Colonel Bobdillo didn't offer to shake hands, which was something of a relief. The little man had set his senses a quivering, and St. Cyprian felt like a hound scenting a bear. Bobdillo was definitely 'in the business' as the saying went. Though in just what capacity St. Cyprian couldn't say.

"Ah. I've heard of you. Thomas' boy-in-the-back," Colonel Bobdillo murmured. St. Cyprian blinked, uncertain of whether offense had been intended. The old man looked at the chalk circle drawn on the floorboards and quirked an eyebrow. "Thomas Carnacki, I mean. Smart chap. Bit daft, but smart. Are you a smart chap, St. Cyprian?"

Something about the way he asked the question put St. Cyprian's teeth on edge. Nonetheless, he smiled and said, "According to some."

Colonel Bobdillo smiled thinly. "Perhaps we shall put that to the test, at some future date. My card, sir," he said, presenting a thin white rectangle to St. Cyprian. As he did so, St. Cyprian noticed a tattoo on the side of his hand, nearly hidden by his thumb. Before he could see it clearly, Bobdillo retracted his hand. "Feel free to call upon me, should you wish, when you are finished with...whatever this is." He snapped his fingers and turned, spreading his arms. "But not tonight! Tonight is for a more entertaining form of magic—but first, the best meal Mayfair has to offer." He swept forward in his curious bobbing way, ushering the others out of the bedroom.

Gallowglass whistled. "Funny geezer, weren't he?"

"Yes, quite," St. Cyprian said, still puzzled. He looked down at the card Bobdillo had given him. It was white with Bobdillo's name and address in Seven Dials, picked out in gold. Besides these there was a highly stylized symbol.

"Is that supposed to be Cleopatra's Needle?" Gallowglass said, peering around his arm at the card he held. "Looks like an obelisk. Only it's got wings."

"Symbolism, innit," he said, mimicking her cadence. He slid the card into his pocket. "Let's get cracking, shall we? This ghost ain't going to dashed well call itself forth, now is it?"

CHAPTER THREE

THE GHOST OF CLARIDGE'S

St. Cyprian prepared himself with an ease born of altogether too much practice. He murmured the first six lines of the Edney incantation and scraped crooked fingers through the air before him, drawing the odd angles of the Voorish sign. One was spoiled for choice when one wanted to see the unseen, but there were far fewer ways of doing so without endangering oneself. As he marked the aether with word and gesture, he took up his place within the circle Gallowglass had marked out. She'd finished the last of the necessary sigils, and he'd anointed the air with the oil of Hyssop. That left only the words, and the bait.

Calling a ghost always required an inducement of some sort. Blood was the traditional medium, heralded by the greatest Greek philosophers and Turkish sorcerers. The dead were always hungry, always cold. A drip of hot blood stirred them up quick as wasps, and set them to speaking. Without blood, they weren't half as likely to speak. Even with it, they were often reluctant. He hoped this spirit, whoever it was, had some message it wished to impart. It always made things easier, when both parties were working towards a common goal.

"Stand back. And try to remain inconspicuous. You have the oil?"

"Got it. And I know what to do," Gallowglass said. "Still wish we'd brought the Pentacle though." The Electric Pentacle had been one of Carnacki's greatest additions to the armoury of the Royal Occultist—a device capable of standing firm against even the most horrific of spirits. Unfortunately, for all its power, it was prone to blowing a fuse at the most inopportune time.

"It's still smashed up after that business in Scarborough," he said. "We'll just have to muddle along the old fashioned way." He took the tip of his thumb between his teeth and bit down hard. Wincing, he extended his arm and squeezed out several drops of bright red blood onto the floor. Then he began to recite the Nuctemeron of Apollonius, albeit in English, rather than Greek. Given Houdini's description of the ghost, St. Cyprian thought that it would respond better to what he suspected was its mother tongue.

"Vouchsafe to be present, O' Father of All, and thou Thrice Mighty Hermes, Conductor of the Dead. Asclepius, son of Hephaistus, Patron of the Healing Art; and thou Osiris, Lord of Strength and Vigour, do thou thyself be present too. Arnebascenis, Patron of Philosophy and yet again Asclepius, son of Imuthe, who presides over poetry. Guide that soul we seek hither, oh Wise Anubis, oh Gentle Hermes..." he recited. As he did so, the air turned at first sour, and then cold.It was as if someone had opened a window on a blustery winter day.

The cold filled the room, and his breath frosted the air. Spirits of all shapes and sizes were suddenly clustered about the circumference of his circle, jostling one another in an attempt to get close. His thumb ached and he squeezed a few more drops of blood onto the floor, causing agitation among the dead, whose numbers were still growing.

They rose from the floor and dripped from the ceiling, expelled themselves from the plaster on the walls and up from between the floorboards. Men and women, old and young, drawn up from the sea of centuries. There were lace collars and top hats, bodices and braces, Roman cuirasses and Saxon cloaks. London was old and full of ghosts, and they could smell blood on the air as clearly as a shark in water.

Foggy hands pawed at the edges of his circle, trying in vain to break it. He could hear Gallowglass behind him, murmuring a quiet prayer. The ghosts wouldn't harm her. They only wanted the blood. They mouthed silent pleas and curses, hollow eyes fixed on his bleeding thumb. He scanned the hungry ranks, seeking the entity Houdini had described.

It took him a moment, but when St. Cyprian saw him, he wondered why he hadn't noticed him earlier. The man was among the most solid of the gathered spectres, and more vibrant than the others, despite the emptiness in his torso. His clothes were almost two decades out of date, and he clutched an umbrella in one ethereal hand. A crimson murk occupied his chest, as if he'd been cored out and left hollow. He alone didn't push at the circle. Instead, he stared at St. Cyprian, his face twisted into a mask of grotesque sorrow. The ghost's mouth opened, and the flickering redness in his chest flared.

I...Phillimore...must...warn...door...open...

St. Cyprian took a breath to steady himself, as the words echoed hollow in his mind. Conan Doyle had been right. The ghost had a message to deliver. But the next bit was the tricky part. Carefully, he smeared blood on his palm.

Then he slowly extended his hand towards the watching ghost.

As his hand breached the circle, the other spirits clustered about it like leeches, mouths opening far too wide, becoming black maws. His skin prickled as dampness enveloped his fingers. With his other hand, he signalled Gallowglass.

She stepped forward, and scattered droplets of the oil of Hyssop on the floor before him. Ghosts reeled back, like animals shying away from fire. St. Cyprian thrust his hand forward, before they could regroup, and brushed his fingers across the insubstantial glow within the chest of his prey. Where the blood touched the spectral clothing, it became semi-solid, and St. Cyprian caught a handful of mouldering cloth and crumbling buttons.

Cold shot through his arm and his fingers went numb. But he had his quarry. He retracted his arm, pulling the ghost towards him, step by step. The entity flickered in his grip, wavering and then growing solid again. The ghost looked about like a man newly awakened from sleep, and he caught at St. Cyprian's arm with fingers like icy talons.

At the moment of contact, the ghost's muttered words became a disjointed flood of images and impressions. They flashed across the surface of St. Cyprian's mind, one after the next, almost too quickly for him to follow. He heard the clatter of carriage wheels across cobblestones, and the voices of vegetable-barrow men. He saw a drawing room, filled with a clutter at once familiar and alien. He smelled a strong tobacco and heard the scratch of a pencil nub across the page of a moleskin notebook. The impressions came faster—he saw robed, animal-headed figures striding across the Embankment in the dead of night. He saw them kneeling before an indistinct shape that might have been Cleopatra's Needle. He heard voices, raised in alarm and anger, and felt the burn in his lungs as he ran. *The three-lobed, burning eye...the door swings wide...He Who Waits...and that of which he is the merest forepaw...*

Blackness rose up around him all of a sudden, and the cold grew worse, freezing the air in his lungs. He could hear the snap of great wings in the distance, and over the ghost's shoulder, he could see three lights, faint but growing brighter. Terribly bright. The lights spun and the sound of wings deafened him. The ghost contorted in his grip, limbs twisting like tendrils of smoke being drawn through a flue.

Must warn him...as the other tried to warn me...warn him...WARN HIM...

"Warn who? Who are you?" St. Cyprian called out, fighting against that inexorable pull. The ghost writhed like a serpent, human shape pulled all out of joint, reduced to a monstrous elasticity. A face like pulled taffy mouthed a name. Startled, St. Cyprian released his hold. The ghost moaned once, loud, low, and long. And then, it was gone.

Shaking, St. Cyprian staggered to the bed and sat down. The numbness in his limbs was fading, as was the ache in his thumb. The other spirits were gone, driven away by whatever force had claimed the soul of his quarry. "Well...this is a rum do and no mistake."

"What? Why?" Gallowglass asked. "What happened? Who was he?"

"Mr. James Phillimore," St. Cyprian said, softly. He shook himself and stood, trying to recover his equilibrium.

143

His spirit still shuddered at the touch of whatever had torn Phillimore from him. "Or so it claimed, at any rate." He looked at Gallowglass. "I could be wrong."

"Sadly, you are not," a voice said, from behind them. They whirled, Gallowglass turning the air blue with her curses. She had her revolver out, but before she could fire, a walking stick swatted the weapon from her hand.

"Ow! Bugger," she yelped.

"Yes, quite," the old man said, as he lowered his stick. "Forgive me. Old habits die hard." He was a bent figure, stick thin and hawk-nosed. The walking stick snaked out and scuffed at the chalk. "Necromancy?" St. Cyprian suspected that it wasn't a question.

"What's it to you?" Gallowglass said, rubbing her hand. St. Cyprian was impressed, despite himself. The old man had gotten into the suite and the bedroom without alerting them. *Though, we were a tad distracted, I will admit*. He shied away from the thought of that terrible shadow. There had been a terrible strength there—a power far greater than any he could recall ever facing.

"Both more and less than you might imagine," the old man said. "Egyptian, though I suspect you learned your English from an Irishman. You spent time in France, as well. And...the Philippines, I believe?"

Gallowglass' eyes widened. The old man smiled. "Several of your curses were of distinctly Tagalog origin. My name is Basil. James Basil. Captain Basil."

"Is it now?" St. Cyprian murmured. He glanced at Gallowglass, who grinned.

"Sounds like a porky to me," she said.

"What's in a name, really?" the old man said, his smile

narrowing to razor thinness. "What matters is what happens next. Where is Houdini?"

"Gone," St. Cyprian said. "A performance, I believe."

"For Colonel Bobdillo?" Basil said. He frowned. "Then I'm too late. I'd thought to warn them, but....You must get to them, and quickly. The Houdinis are in great danger. The Door of Eternal Night yawns wide, and unless it is closed, what waits beyond it will claim Houdini the way it claimed the unfortunate James Phillimore."

"The door of...what are you talking about?" St. Cyprian said. "Now see here, if you know something about this I'd be obliged if you shared the pipe, gaffer." He took a step towards the old man, who looked at him sadly.

"Later," he said. "But for now, you must go. And swiftly—the lives of the Houdinis are at stake and you and your assistant may be the only ones capable of seeing them safely out of it."

"How? We don't even know where they've—wait," St. Cyprian began. He snapped his fingers. "Eureka! Of course, the card." He snatched the card Colonel Bobdillo had given him out of his pocket and examined it. "Seven Dials. That's where they'll be. We can take our motor car."

The old man was gone.

Preview
Dead West: West of Pale
By J. Patrick Allen

*An exclusive preview of the new novel by J. Patrick Allen,
picking up where his Pulp Ark New Pulp Awards (2016)
nominated story left off. West of Pale is due April 1st, 2016*

Chapter One
The Thing that Waits

Father woke me in the night with a hand clamped over my
mouth. Through the shining moonlight I could see he was
not looking at me, but rather out the window. In his other
hand he held his Sharps buffalo rifle. Light and shadow
threw contrast over his face, hiding his eyes but showing
every nervous twitch of his jaw and beard.

"Get up," he whispered. I can still recall the spicy
tobacco smell of his breath, the quivering fear in his voice.
"No—slowly, son. Slowly, and keep low."

Following his instructions I slid out of bed on the far
side of the window and hid behind it. Crouching, he led me
away from the bed, backing up against the wardrobe.
Outside I heard a snuffling, grunting noise. Some kind of
animal, though what would make noises like that? The
snuffling could have been an armadillo, but for the volume
and depth of noise it produced. The grunting could have
been a frog, but for the size of the sound. What ever it was,
it had to be the size of a man, and the thought put lead in
my gut.

For a brief moment as the noise approached I feared I'd see something truly hideous appear at the window. I sunk a little lower behind the bed. During the day I might brag to the other boys of my bravery, but that was day and this was night.

According to the stories father told me the night time is the time for horrors. For packs of wolves out of the woods. For witches who roam the forest in their gingerbread houses, looking for disobedient children to eat. For fairies that make wicked bargains the mortal always regrets in the end. The night belongs to monsters.

The sound crossed around the corner, beyond the window and I felt father beside me relax a little. He motioned with his head for the wardrobe. Obeying I got in and he pushed me to the back, covering me with jackets and hung britches and shirts. For good measure he propped two open boxes of moth balls on the floor of the wardrobe.

Father rested a hand on my cheek, studying me by moonlight. "If I do not come for you by the morning, there is a secret compartment in the desk. Third of the small drawers, a false bottom."

"Yes, father." If he didn't come for me? Where would he be? Surely the animal could not get in the house.

"You are my son, Charlie." His voice broke at the end. I saw a single tear run a wet track down his cheek. He closed the wardrobe door and shut me into darkness. In with the smell of clothes, lye soap, and moth balls. In there, where the sound of my own frightened breathing almost drowned out the sound of him walking away.

A little light flared in the crack of the door. Father had lit a lamp. Just then the house shook. From above me a moth ball tumbled off a shelf and into my shoulder. I had to bite my hand not to scream.

Again the house rattled, and I realized what I was hearing. Something pounding the door. After a moment I heard the sound of glass shattering.

A new voice, gnarled and wheezy, shouted "You're mine, first born!"

Over my own labored breathing I heard the sound of father's Sharps go off. An animal roar pierced the night, followed by my father's own tortured screams. Just as suddenly as it started his screams were cut off. I heard something heavy – a body – drop to the floor, and something let out an asthmatic hiss.

That something was tumbled about the parlor. I heard furniture disturbed, glass knocked from shelves. And then it was over. I waited for father to come back. He never did.

When I could see the first rays of sunlight streaming between the wardrobe doors I pushed myself out. Cool morning air hit my face, and I could feel the air especially against my wet cheeks. I stumbled outside and behind the house. It was past the vegetable garden that I found the blood. A trail of blood led off for the woods and the air carried a hint of the river stink of fish and urine.

My gut lurched at the smell and the sight of the blood. If there were anything in my stomach I might have lost it then. As it was I fell to my knees and retched. I spent several minutes there, my shoulders and gut clenching, waiting for the heaves to subside. When I was recovered enough I followed the trail like the crimson brush stroke of a gigantic painter.

The morning sun was not yet high enough to chase off the dark of the woods. Blue light mingled with black tree shadows and spots of dark mud. The morning birds were just beginning their song and somewhere distant a wood pecker hunted for breakfast.

Perhaps it was fear, perhaps it was the unusual situation I found myself in, but I felt eyes in those woods. My head cast this way and that, looking over my shoulder in search of the unseen watcher, all the while I kept an eye on the trail. The blood led to the muddy banks of the Missouri. The stain vanished among the rich dark mud, but a track dragged through it and down to the water. I found one of father's boots caught on a rock.

Numb, I walked home. My mind could not process what had happened. I like to believe it was shock. What ever it was was sufficient to see me carried back to the house.

There, the Constable and his boy awaited me.

"Little Charlie," he smiled to me. The constable's son Martin ignored me – we were not close.

I said nothing, could say nothing. Something caught in my throat so I forced myself to nod in greeting.

"Where is Florian?" Constable Haak asked. I did not meet his eyes. He took stock of me – of the front door knocked off its hinges, of the broken window, and he nodded.

"I see. I'm here because Frau Blucher said there had been gunshots last night. Do you know anything about this?" He eyed the boot in my hand.

He waited for me, patient, while I found my voice. When at last it came to me I said, "Someone has killed him, sir." It was a small voice, quiet and gravelly. It hardly sounded like my own. "I followed the trail to the river."

"Do you know who did it?"

I shrugged, lost.

Constable Haak conducted a cursory investigation of the house. The smell of fish in the place caused Martin to blanch. The constable noted the disturbed living room, the bullet hole in the wall, and the discarded Sharps. After, he inspected the trail leading to the river. He said nothing to me, but I heard him a room over conferring with his son.

"An animal," he said. "It looks like an animal did this."

I did not agree.

He found me a moment later, sitting on the edge of the bed I had shared with father, staring at the open wardrobe. Constable Haak laid a hand on my shoulder and told me of his findings.

Florian Kirchner, my father, was gone from this world. He had gone on to join the Father and I would not see him again until the end of my days. You must have some sympathy, as even one who is not a boy of thirteen would have done as I did. I turned and I cried. The Constable was kind enough to offer me his shoulder, and to offer to let me stay with him for a time. This was not the last offer I would receive. Behind his father I saw Martin frown. It was not the last offer I would turn down.

While he sat with me his boy went back on up the hill to town, and by the time the churches chimed noon local townswomen were stopping by to see to me. Each of course offered to let me stay with them until I could find my feet again. Frau Sackoff's offer was the most tempting, as she ran a boarding house and I could have a space of my own instead of insinuating myself on another family—a happy family. And she was kind enough to help me when the mortician came to perform his bleak duties.

When evening came on I managed to urge the crowd that had formed in my father's house to leave for the evening. And there I was, alone. I stared at a small picture of my father put up on the mantle place. He held mother's hand. I do not remember much of her, but I had memorized the details of that photograph as I grew up. Now I turned my eye to him as well. He looked like me in so many ways. I had mother's long nose, but had inherited his sandy hair and brown eyes. When I felt like I could not look at the picture without crying again I turned away.

In that moment, in that time, the world ceased to seem rational. Along the bookshelves were a modest collection of science books, medical books, nature books—a legacy from Florian Kirchner, who wanted his son Charles to know the spiritual and literal wealth that knowledge could bring. The world was not rational. The world was a place of monsters. Father's words returned to me – the desk. I crossed the room to it and pulled out the third drawer. Turning the drawer bottom up I gave it three hard raps on the desk top. On the third knock the false bottom fell out and papers came with.

Folded documents fell to the desk, scattering. It took me a moment of sifting through documents—the deed for the house, father and mother's immigration documents, a poem—to find what it was he must have been referring to. I unfolded a scrap of paper to find an unfamiliar man's angular, cramped writing.

thank you for the help
if your ever in trouble find this address & ask for
Samuel Clayton
- SHC

The address listed was in Kentucky; Elizabethtown—a place unfamiliar to me. It was something to think on. Why would my father recommend this Samuel Clayton to me? Who was this man, and why did I not know him myself? The name was obviously not German, so he would not be one of the towns folk. I tucked the letter and the address away in my pocket.

It was in my pocket that the papers stayed, through the funeral service the next day. It was at my bed side during the nights when I thought I could hear something stalking outside the house waiting for me (and a moment later it was with me in the wardrobe, hiding). And it was in my pocket when three days after I lost father I finally accepted Frau Sackoff's offer to let me stay at her boarding house.

I moved in to a small room at the top of her three story brick house, feeling safer even as I took a small bed in the corner of the attic. It's easy to feel afraid when you are alone and in the dark. It is much harder to feel afraid when you can feel and hear the presence of people about you.

That night I lay up, staring at the shifting shadows cast through the window by the moon and the trees. I thought I could hear something moving about outside, looking for me. Waiting for me. It stalked circles about the house for perhaps a few hours until I heard it no longer.

When the noise ended my pulse returned. I withdrew the note from the pocket of my trousers hanging on the back of a chair and read through it for the hundredth time. The way

I saw it, I had two choices: Stay here and wait to be pulled into the river, or find the man who wrote this letter.

Really, there was only one choice.